Priestess

Eturuvie Erebor

A DOZ Chronicles Romance Series

ISBN: 978-1-8383844-6-3

PRIESTESS

Published in London, England by Eturuvie Erebor trading as DOZ Chronicles, a unit of DOZ Network.

Bound by fate.

Divided by their different worlds.

In the end, love is a choice...

One still night, Tiyan's consciousness is no longer entirely her own. Somewhere between the realms of sleep and waking, a man enters—a stranger whose presence feels oddly familiar. When she meets him in reality, the connection is instant—Usi is powerful, loving, and knows exactly what he wants. But he is also a traditional man, the Chief Priest of Benin and Tiyan would have to step into the coveted–but weighty–role of priestess.

Usi, the revered Chief Priest, has kept a lifelong vow of celibacy, his body consecrated to the gods. But as a force more powerful than tradition begins to stir within him, he knows his time for love has come. His night encounter with Tiyan only tells him what he already knows–she is the one. But certainty doesn't come so easily to Tiyan. Usi's world is one of ancient beliefs and heavy expectations—nothing like life as she knows it.

With their conflicting beliefs, responsibilities, and cultures pulling them in opposite directions, Usi and Tiyan must decide if their love is worth weathering the pressures of destiny, tradition, and those who would do anything to see them fail.

Dear Reader,

Thank you for reading the stories of Eki, Ede and Amenze as captured in the novels, *Oloi: A Queen Shrouded in Mystery*, *Ede* and *Olori*. This is Tiyan's story and initially, I had no intention of writing it. I was content to have it embedded in the love stories of Eki and Osad and Ede and Sato. But as I wrote the story of Amenze and Bawo and also began to consider the possibility of taking the series to television, the desire to flesh out Tiyan and Usi's incredible love story grew, and it became imperative to tell their story.

It is a beautiful love story. I am sure you will agree with me. I have enjoyed writing it and hope you'll enjoy reading it.

I would love to hear your thoughts, so don't hesitate to share them. You can write to me through my website, www.eturuvieerebor.com, or via my email eturuvie@eturuvieerebor.com.

I look forward to hearing from you.

Evie.

For Linda "Lindoski"

For my nephew Aaron

Special thanks to my community of readers, especially the askers of, "When is your next book out?"

CHAPTER ONE

Chief Usi Isekhure was restless. His plan for an early night had been disrupted by his inability to relax. Climbing out of the luxurious king-size bed, he slipped his feet into a pair of white bedroom slippers, slipped a white dressing robe over his white piped cotton pyjamas, and stepped outside onto his private balcony through the wide double glass sliding doors. Outside in the cool of the night, overlooking the city which lay below the mountain top where he lived, he paced.

It was time for him to marry. The anticipation grew intolerable with each passing day. As a young man preparing for the role of chief priest, he committed to celibacy. His commitment to abstaining from sexual intercourse allowed him to be tuned in to the gods of the land, hearing from them and speaking as their oracle when commanded.

He understood the vital importance of marrying a Benin woman who comprehended the culture and the significance of his role as chief priest. A woman who had kept herself pure and would one day carry the next Chief Priest of the Benin Kingdom in her womb.

He had not met such a woman. However, he hadn't looked, had he? While living in America, he hadn't taken the initiative to search for a wife, convinced that the timing wasn't suitable and unsure if he would encounter a Benin woman willing to accompany him back to Benin to reside there once his father passed away, and he became chief priest.

It had now been over two years since he left his life and job as a stockbroker in New York and returned to live in Benin following his father's death and his subsequent assumption into the office of the chief priest. There had been ample time to seek a spouse, but he hadn't. Perhaps he expected the gods to handpick a wife for him. He laughed mirthlessly. That seemed unlikely. It had not happened with his forebears, who had occupied the office before him; it would unlikely happen with him.

Usually, when the gods picked a wife, they chose one for a king, and the chief priest bore such a message as he had done with Eki Alile, Chief Alile's daughter, who the gods chose to marry Crown Prince Osad Edoni of the Benin Kingdom. But he would pick a wife for himself.

Halting, he turned northward and let out a sigh. His gaze ascended to the sky. Where was she? No doubt, out there somewhere, waiting to be discovered by him. He would find her soon. The wait was becoming unbearable. The wait was…

Wait a minute.

What was this that he was seeing?

The cloud grew dark, as if ready to pour. Nothing unusual about that. With the Benin Kingdom situated in the tropics, torrential downpours were not only common but usually preceded by thick, dark clouds. Except this cloud was different. This cloud signalled something was about to occur—something ominous, something dreadful.

He stepped back into the house and hurried into his private shrine. Opening a bottle of gin, he poured out a libation to the gods and his ancestors, assuming a posture he used in sacred rites. He lost count of the time he stayed in that pose, but it swiftly became apparent what was unfolding. He stood up and returned outside. The sky showed no sign of clearing. The dark clouds remained looming over the kingdom.

He pulled out his phone and dialled a number he had not called in years. He last called the number while under his father's tutelage, learning what it took to be chief priest. His father thoroughly educated him, sharing all his knowledge and ensuring he would always be prepared for anything. The adversary was about to learn this.

"What do you think you are doing?" he inquired sharply as soon as the older man answered the phone. He might be younger, but holding the office of the chief priest made his age irrelevant. He was the gods' mouthpiece.

"Chief Isekhure, I greet you!" The older man's voice was

gruff and drained.

"You bring an omen to my door and tell me you greet me?"

"Chief Isekhure, I am not ignorant of the matter you speak of. But believe me when I tell you, the matter is out of my hands."

Usi frowned. "What do you mean?"

"The palace guards require me to attend the palace for some interrogation."

"You should have informed the guards about your prohibition from setting foot in the city and that ancient laws have banished you to remain in Ugoneki."

Laughter echoed on the line. "You think I left Ugoneki without explaining this situation to the guards?"

"I don't know what to think; frankly, what I think is irrelevant. The cloud's thickness and darkness show you're a few kilometres from the city gate. You must return now!"

"If I could, I would, Chief Isekhure."

"Give the phone to the guard closest to you."

These native security agents, who had neither knowledge nor regard for ancient laws and customs, made him sick. They made his work as chief priest a nightmare. They were bringing evil into the city with them, and it would be his responsibility to cleanse the land of the omen while they slept in their beds, oblivious to the havoc they had wrecked.

There was some background noise, and an unfamiliar voice joined the conversation. He did not know the owner, nor did he care. Without delay, he passed on the message as he received it from the gods.

"You will not bring that man into this city. The ancient laws and customs forbid it. If you need to interrogate him, you will do so anywhere you choose but outside the city's gates. There is no kingdom with two kings. Use your tongue to count your teeth. I would hate to use your head to appease the gods. My name is Isekhure!"

He ended the call and stood back, hands clasped behind his back, watching the sky. No change occurred. It meant the procession with the undesirable individual continued to advance towards the city gate. He shut his eyes and opened them in the spirit, and he saw the Benin *Iya*, the ancient walls of the kingdom that separated the city from smaller towns in the kingdom.

The procession advanced towards the west gate. He exhaled and began a spiritual journey, intending to reach the gate before they did. Instantly, the vehicles stopped, turned around toward Ugoneki, and the clouds receded.

He heaved a sigh of relief even as he made a mental note to perform the requisite land cleansing in the coming days. With the problem resolved, thoughts of his future wife once again consumed him.

When would he find her? When he found her, would she understand the life he led? The life predetermined for him before birth? Would she accept it? Would she consent to be his priestess?

He turned and proceeded indoors. Settled in bed, he closed his eyes and exhaled. Who was she?

***

Tiyan stifled a yawn as she rode in the back of a minicab laden with shopping bags. After a long day, she craved her bed. She glanced out the window at the teeming crowds of locals and tourists and the major department stores and brand leaders Oxford Street was famous for. After spending most of the day wandering around Marble Arch, Oxford Street, and West End, she found no interest in the sight before her.

She wondered if there was a shop on Oxford Street that they hadn't visited as they verified if the summer sale advertised in the shop window was authentic or a tactic to attract customers. She stifled another yawn. Fortunately, she had no plan to go out tonight. She couldn't, possibly. Not when she struggled to keep her eyes open.

She'd travelled on vacation with her cousins, Eki and

Aisosa, fondly called Aiai, and her best friend Amenze. They travelled to Dubai, Paris, and now London. It had been an exhilarating but draining experience. She had not fully recovered from the jetlag. They had arrived in Dubai, seen the sights, shopped, window-shopped, and eaten out. Barely getting any rest, they rose early and got into bed late.

They hopped on the plane to Paris, repeating the pattern. In London now, sleep deprivation took its toll on her. Perhaps not the others, as evidenced by their chatting and giggling in the back of the minicab on the way home. They kept the driver entertained from the moment they climbed into the taxi. She was eager to reach Aiai's vacation home in Chislehurst and sink into the comfort of her bed.

"Cousin T, want to watch a movie?" Eki asked as they trudged upstairs to their bedrooms carrying their shopping bags.

"No!" Tiyan protested. "I can barely keep my eyes open."

"We'll order pizza," Amenze said. "The mighty meaty with the stuffed crust that you love."

"I don't care!" Tiyan grumbled. "You all enjoy your movie and pizza. I am going to bed."

"Leave Cousin T to go to bed. She's sleep-deprived and is like a bear with a sore head. She'll only ruin our movie night," Aiai called out to the girls from downstairs.

Tiyan hurriedly changed into her nightwear, brushed her teeth, and cleaned her face. The bed looked inviting, and she counted the minutes until she climbed in between the sheets and placed her tired head on the soft pillows.

As she climbed into bed, her phone rang, and her irritation rose as she recognised the number. What was his problem? Why did he keep bothering her?

"Mr Orobator, I told you I would be travelling. I am not in Benin. Whatever you want to discuss will have to wait until I return!" She didn't give him a chance to speak. She cut the call and switched off her phone.

What a louse, she thought as she punched her pillows furiously to arrange them. Ekpen Orobator gave her the creeps. Hopefully, he wouldn't give her nightmares.

She lay nestled in bed, on the verge of sleep, when the sound of his entrance into her bedroom stirred her. He stood inside her room, just a few feet from the double bed. She held her breath and stilled herself for what would follow.

Her eyes were closed, yet she could feel his presence drawing near, causing her heartbeat to quicken. Her heart pounded so fiercely that she feared it might leap out of her chest.

The mattress shifted under his weight as he climbed into the bed with her. She remained still, afraid to even breathe. He removed the sheet that covered her, exposing her body clad in the pink silk nightie to his eyes and touch. She felt exposed, and a chill ran down her spine, reminding her that despite it being summer, the temperature had dropped slightly because it was nighttime. She needed that sheet to shield herself from his intense gaze, which she sensed moving all over her. Her body trembled ever so slightly, and she needed the sheet to keep warm.

Then he touched her, his hand on the small of her back, pulled her closer to him. The softness of her body touched the male hardness of his, and Tiyan experienced her whole body erupt in flames. A desire stronger than anything she had ever known engulfed her, threatening to consume her.

She wanted him. She wanted this man, this intruder. Whoever he may be.

The hand resting on her back was not repulsive. It did not leave her disgusted as she had thought. A man's touch usually left her repulsed. Following a negative experience with one man at the age of seventeen, she developed a deep dislike for being touched or kissed. A reason she'd shied away from dating as an undergraduate and even while doing her master's degree. She wouldn't think about that negative experience or its perpetrator. She would lose herself in the man with her whose touch made her yearn for more.

But how can this be? She argued with herself. No man had

ever elicited such a response from her. How had this man done it? How did he make her go up in flames with one touch? Without pondering too deeply, she knew the answer. This man was different.

He was no stranger to her. His hand on the small of her back wasn't the hand of a stranger. It caressed her in a familiar way. The hand belonged to a lover. A lover who knew every inch of her body. A lover who understood when and how to touch her. She thought it strange because she'd never had a lover.

His mouth found hers and moved expertly over it. She parted her lips, granting him access, powerless to stop him, *not wanting* to stop him. Then, when she would have wrapped her arms around his neck and pulled him closer, and when she would have angled her head and deepened the kiss, he broke the kiss and pulled away.

Stunned and unable to believe what had just transpired, she opened her eyes and backed away in horror as she realised who it was.

"Chief Isekhure!" Tiyan exclaimed as she jumped out of sleep, flicking on the bedside lamp.

She looked around her as a chill travelled down her spine. The encounter had seemed so real. Nothing like a dream at all. It had appeared like he had been right inside her bedroom, lying next to her on the bed, touching her, kissing her. But that was absurd. She wasn't even in the exact location as the Chief Priest of the Benin Kingdom. Besides, what business did he have with her?

He had visited her home multiple times to see her uncle, Chief Alile, who had assumed a paternal role for her after her father's passing when she was only thirteen years old. But they had never met. She knew of him. Which Benin person didn't? But he was no friend or acquaintance. Why did she dream about him? Why did he touch her intimately as a man touched his betrothed or wife?

With no answers, and her head pounding, Tiyan decided to return to sleep. She picked up the bottle of water on the bedside table and drank a good portion of it, hoping it would help with the throbbing in her head. Then she rearranged her pillows and lay back, shutting her eyes. Whatever the dream meant or didn't mean, time would tell. She had a strong conviction about that. This had been no accident.

CHAPTER TWO

Usi opened his eyes, smiling. She had to be the most beautiful woman he had ever set eyes on. Slender, with long arms and limbs, she had thick natural hair that cascaded past her shoulders and skin that was soft and smooth. Exquisite, delicate, and his. His smile broadened as he reflected on her responsiveness to his touch and kiss. Indeed, she proved to be the ideal match for him. His woman. Finally. All he had to do was wait to meet her in person.

He had a photographic memory and would recognise her whenever he saw her. Longingly, he prayed for the gods to hasten that day. He grew increasingly impatient. Restless. His body craved release. The sooner he met her and married her, the better.

The sudden vibrating of his mobile phone on the bedside table interrupted his thoughts. He turned his head even as his hand reached for the irritating device. The number seemed unfamiliar, but he sensed the call originated from the palace and it related to the king. His heartbeat quickened slightly.

"Isekhure," he said, offering no salutation. His voice warned the person on the line to tread cautiously.

"Greetings, Chief," the caller sounded like the king's head servant. "Sir, it's the king, he–"

"Think before you speak!" Usi barked the order, cutting the other man off. "I am on my way!"

He got out of bed. He'd got little sleep, yet he was accustomed to it. Being chief priest and the kingdom's watchman required him to stay awake regularly, communing with the gods while the kingdom slept. He hurried into his shrine, poured out a libation to the gods, and took his prayer staff in his hand, shutting his eyes and muttering an incantation as he did.

Moments later, he opened his eyes. Nothing remained to be done. The gods had spoken. The great white chalk had been broken.

Oba gha to kpèrè! Long live the king! Long live Omo N'Oba N'Edo Uku-akpolokpolo, Oba Edoni I of the Benin Kingdom!

He left the shrine and entered his bathroom. A few minutes later, dressed in a traditional white shirt embroidered with the *Ada and Eben* royal sceptres, a plain white wrapper and white shoes, he ran down the white marble stairs with white wrought-iron bannisters that led into the grand foyer. Then he exited the double glass doors to the front of the house, where his driver pulled up in the white BMW X7.

"*Uruese.* Thank you," Usi said as he got behind the wheel and turned the vehicle toward the electronically controlled gate.

The kingdom remained partially asleep as he drove to the

palace. Partially asleep and oblivious to the change already taking place. He had long sensed the impending need for change, yet remained silent. It had not been his obligation to make such an announcement. Indeed, the king himself possessed the ability to comprehend such things.

He arrived at the king's residence, where the head servant waited to usher him straight to the king's bedroom. The king's physician, also a member of the council of chiefs, had been called and stood by the king, who lay in bed. The king appeared to be sleeping peacefully. Indeed, he was. Usi looked at the doctor, Chief Bazuaye, and held his gaze briefly. They exchanged no words. No words needed to be exchanged.

"Thank you for being here, Doctor Bazuaye," Usi spoke in a hushed voice. "You don't need to be told that no word leaves this room." He looked from the doctor to the head servant. Both bowed to demonstrate their loyalty.

"His Majesty will not be moved." He continued addressing both men, who nodded their heads in agreement. "I need to make a phone call to Crown Prince Osad Edoni, after which I will determine the performance of certain traditional rites. You both may wait in His Majesty's sitting room adjoining the bedroom. I will go into his study and make my phone call there."

Without waiting for a response, he walked briskly out of

the room. It was going to be a long and busy day, marking the start of a hectic few weeks. He wished it this way. This way, his attention would be diverted from his woman, and he would regain control over his body, as he preferred.

***

"Tiyan, do you also have plans to add a DBA to your MBA?"

Tiyan dragged herself away from her thoughts and looked at the young man sitting beside her in the exquisite Thai restaurant. He was her date for the evening: Alexander Papadopoulos, a cousin to Dimitris Papadopoulos, Amenze's boyfriend.

She frowned, wondering why he would ask her such a question. What had brought that on? Had she missed something? Likely.

"A DBA?" she asked, feeling foolish for not knowing how the conversation had progressed before his question.

Amenze gave her a gentle kick under the table and a look that warned her to behave.

"Amenze was just telling us of her plans to add a DBA to her, just concluded MBA," Dimitris said.

Was she? Tiyan remembered nothing.

She smiled her thanks at Dimitris and turned to Alexander. “Oh, no. I don’t have plans to do a DBA. Not for the foreseeable future. I think for now I am quite satisfied with the MBA I have bagged besides my accounting degree.”

She picked up her glass of water and took a sip, relieved she hadn’t been called out for zoning out. And she’d been zoning out as her mind frequently drifted back to her dream last night. Suppose it could be called that. She had no idea what to call it and had told no one about it. What would she tell them? That Chief Usi Isekhure, the chief priest, and the most revered man in Benin apart from the monarch, had come to her bedroom and made love to her?

It was unthinkable—not how he had accessed her bedroom, but why he would want to. She lacked recognition or importance. Why would Chief Isekhure take any interest in her? He was rich; his father before him and his grandfather before his father had been wealthy chief priests.

He attended school in America. Indeed, he would pick a Benin girl from an affluent or upper-middle-class home. She lived as an orphan under the care of her uncle, who occupied a lower middle-class status and, despite his position as a chief, often faced exclusion from the wealthier chiefs in the kingdom.

“I take it then that you’re not as ambitious as Amenze?”

Tiyan smiled, pulling herself from her daydreams and

setting down her glass of water. "I wouldn't say I am not as ambitious as Amenze. We just have different plans."

She switched him off in her head as she again gave her thoughts to Chief Usi Isekhure. Earlier that morning, she researched the young chief priest quickly before going downstairs for breakfast, sightseeing, and shopping with Eki, Amenze, and Aiai. She liked what she had discovered about him. Inexperienced in dating and lacking knowledge about men, she remained oblivious to the feeling of being in love and found it difficult to discern whether she was in love. However, Usi Isekhure met her criteria.

He embodied the type of man she desired for the remainder of her life. The greatest attraction for her being that as chief priest, he was expected to keep his body free of any sexual entanglement until marriage, and as a younger man, he had voluntarily taken a vow of celibacy. He, like her, was a virgin. She'd always wanted a man who had kept himself for her as she'd kept herself for him.

Eki, a hopeless romantic, had assured her that a man who loved her would wait. Amenze, a realist, urged her to open her eyes and observe the real world. How many men were virgins past the age of fifteen?

But Usi was. And he exuded both physical attractiveness and intellectual prowess. He worked as a stockbroker before returning to Benin following his father's passing. Despite being the youngest among the chiefs, he wielded considerable authority and respect within the kingdom, serving as the chief priest and the leader of the council of chiefs. These qualities made him appealing to a girl like her.

She had spent much of the day reflecting on him and their encounter from last night, pondering what it all meant. Consequently, she found herself mostly distracted. While having afternoon tea at The Savoy, Aiai expressed her frustration by snapping at her.

Once again, she let thoughts of the chief priest distract her. She smiled at Alexander, and as he responded with a grin of his own, she quietly hoped he wasn't thinking of seeing her again after tonight. It was a double date with Amenze and Dimitris, so she came along. But that didn't mean she had any plans to see him after tonight.

"So, what are your plans?" Alexander asked, sipping his drink. "Long-term and short-term?"

Tiyan raised a brow. What was this? A job interview? The dude had only met her and wanted to learn about her plans. To see if he fit into them or what?

"I plan to return to my hometown, get a job, or start a business and earn money. That's the short-term plan. The long-term plan is to marry and have a dozen babies. Are you in?"

Amenze burst out laughing, and Dimitris joined her. Alexander turned slightly red under his olive skin as Tiyan grinned at him and nudged him gently with an elbow.

That's what you get when you ask a stranger a personal question, she thought. Usi Isekhure briefly crossed her mind. She would not have minded him asking her about her long-term plans. But only because she liked him and envisaged a future with him. Besides, he had been strangely familiar while lying beside her in bed last night. As if they had been lovers in a past life.

They danced at a Mayfair nightclub after dinner before going back home. Tiyan gladly waved goodbye to the charming Alexander. Despite his attractiveness, she experienced no connection or desire to meet him again. Also, the entire time they danced, she had compared his arm around her waist to Usi's touch the night before. She had known then that a second date would never happen. Thankfully, he reciprocated her feelings and bid her farewell at the end of the evening without requesting another meeting.

CHAPTER THREE

A few days later….

She was the woman from his dream. His woman. He recognised her instantly. In real life, she appeared even more breathtaking. Usi glanced at Chief Alile's daughter, Eki. He saw the striking family resemblance, except his woman had paler skin. Did she happen to be Alile's daughter as well? Why had he never met her despite having been to Alile's house for palace business a few times?

He stared at her because he couldn't help it. A desire to pick her up, carry her to his bedroom, and keep her locked there forever overwhelmed him. Finally, she had appeared, in reality, tangible for him to see, touch, and kiss. He noticed her restlessness, interpreting it as a sign that she was aware of being observed.

She kept her head bowed, and eyes lowered, possibly because of the presence of the next monarch of the Benin Kingdom. But he sensed her shyness and noticed her deliberate avoidance of his gaze. As he kept watching her, completely cut off from his immediate surroundings and the goings-on, she lifted her head and met his gaze. The beauty of her eyes surpassed anything he had witnessed before. She radiated true beauty, was absolutely exquisite, his priestess.

The instant Tiyan raised her head and locked eyes with Usi, she froze, and everything and everyone else in the room faded into the background. The pictures she had seen online didn't do justice to his good looks in person. Standing at over six feet tall, he had a handsome face, a dark complexion, and a lean, muscular physique. Since their recent encounter, he occupied her thoughts incessantly.

The following night, she had retired to bed, excited about the possibility of seeing him again in her dream. How disappointed she'd been when she woke without dreaming of him.

She smiled shyly at him. His eyes narrowed in response. At that moment, she realised their encounter had not been a dream or coincidence. He had sought her out, come into her bedroom, and touched, held, and kissed her.

She knew, Usi reflected. He witnessed the precise moment of realisation in her eyes. Their encounter had been no dream. He urged her to maintain eye contact despite sensing her inclination to avert her gaze in embarrassment.

There's nothing to be embarrassed about, baby. What occurred took place between us.

She continued to hold his gaze, but the enchantment was

shattered when the crown prince called for his attention, sounding somewhat irritated. He forced himself to look away from his beloved wife-to-be, switched off the not-so-sacred thoughts in his head, and gave his attention to Crown Prince Osad Edoni. After all, this meeting revolved around Prince Osad and Chief Alile's daughter, Eki, who were finally meeting following the prophecy of their future marriage.

Osad was far from impressed, but this did not bother Usi. They would marry. The gods had spoken to him. He embodied the qualities of a chief priest who was truly invaluable and genuine.

Usi attempted to be attentive, responsive and engaged. A bright smile spread across his face, his eyes sparkling with delight, as Osad asked everyone to leave the room so he could be alone with Eki. This became a welcome development for Usi, enabling him to chat with his woman. What was she called? He shrugged. This was his chance to find out.

As the servants ushered them into the waiting room adjoining the main reception they had just vacated, Usi moved quickly and intercepted his woman, offering a quick greeting to Chief and Mrs Alile as he did so.

"May I have a quick word, if that's okay?" Guiding her with his hand without letting it touch her, he steered her towards a smaller reception room further along the hall.

"Good afternoon, Chief Isekhure," Tiyan greeted.

"Please, call me Usi. After the other night, we are on a first-name basis. Besides, when I hear Chief Isekhure, I instinctively search for my father."

She smiled, unveiling the most beautiful teeth he had ever seen.

"Alright. Usi it is."

"Good," he said. "But you have the advantage over me. You see, I do not know your name."

"My name is Imuetiyan. Imuetiyan Alile. But everyone calls me Tiyan. Eki calls me Cousin T."

"As you are not my cousin, I will join everyone else in calling you Tiyan or T."

She laughed, and he sensed his body stir. "Fair enough," she said.

"So, I take it you are Chief Alile's niece?" he asked.

"Yes, I am. Uncle Zogie is my father's older brother."

"And your parents, do they live here in Benin?" As the words left his mouth, he got a sixth sense that asking that question was incorrect and mentally kicked himself as her smile turned to sadness.

"My parents and brother died a long time ago. My living

arrangements have been with my uncle and his family since I reached the age of thirteen."

"I am sorry to hear that." He meant it. He'd do anything to erase the sadness and restore that infectious smile and laughter.

She offered a slight smile and nodded in recognition of his condolences.

"Tiyan, I'm confident you are aware of the purpose behind my request for this audience."

Shyly, she smiled and briefly averted her gaze before meeting his eyes. *That's my girl*, he thought to himself.

"I'd like to come and take you out later tonight. We need to get acquainted. Would you like that?"

"Yes. Very much."

"Good," he said with a smile as he handed her his phone to enter her number. "I will call you, but expect me around 7 pm."

"I will," she said.

They returned to the room where the others waited. But before entry, servants arrived to inform them that the crown prince desired everyone to return to the main reception.

As Chief Alile would have walked past him, Usi stopped

him.

"Chief Alile," he greeted.

"Chief Isekhure," Chief Alile replied, smiling. He was perceptive enough to comprehend the situation.

"I won't waste your time, as the crown prince has called us back into his presence. And I won't beat about the bush either. Your niece, Tiyan. She is mine. I will perform the customary rites within one month."

Chief Alile nodded. "First, Tiyan is my daughter. By tradition, she became my daughter the day her father, my brother, died. Second, she has been through a lot, and while I understand your need to marry her quickly, I would like to crave your indulgence to give her some time to get used to the idea of being your wife. You have my permission to woo her. If she appears happy after a few months, do as tradition dictates. I will not stand in the way."

Usi exhaled deeply, reluctant to concede that Chief Alile had a point. "No more than six months, Chief Alile."

Chief Alile bowed slightly. "As you wish, Chief Isekhure."

Tiyan was in a deep reflection as she sat before the mirror in her small bedroom, getting ready for her date with Usi. She was delighted to be seeing him again. A blissful smile spread across her face, radiating warmth. She liked Usi and sensed he was the one. Also, she perceived that the feeling was mutual. Usi Isekhure liked her. This excited her. However, she was worried about Eki.

Over two years ago, Eki was prophesied to marry the crown prince, but he never showed an interest in her. He continually avoided meeting her, and Eki had no reason to feel committed to him. Then, an incident happened a couple of weeks ago.

Eki's immediate older sister was discovered to be pregnant by Odaro, Eki's boyfriend, and set to marry him. Although Odaro had broken up with Eki, while still involved with Eki, he had been having an affair with Eseosa, and as she had become pregnant, he dumped Eki to marry her.

That annoyed Eki, especially as Aunt Ayi, Eki's mother, remained unrepentant about her role in bringing Eseosa and Odaro together. Eki wanted to humiliate her parents and decided to throw her virginity away while on holiday visiting Dubai, Paris, and London. And she had thrown it away.

Three nights ago, on their final vacation night, Eki slept with a man at The Dorchester. Today, after visiting the Edaiken Palace, Tiyan, Amenze, and Aiai discovered that the man Eki slept with was the crown prince. Eki recognised him, but he failed to recognise her. That was not the only problem. He sent word following the meeting that he would marry Eki. Did it mean everything was fine, and the prophecy was about to be fulfilled? No!

Eki was due to have a virginity test at the palace hospital tomorrow morning. Tiyan knew she would fail that test woefully. Chaos would ensue. Despite her ability to persuade everyone, including the crown prince, that he was responsible for deflowering her, the notion of the future queen engaging in a rendezvous at a hotel with a stranger would cause a massive scandal.

The prince would never marry Eki, and the Alile family would be disgraced. Eki desired to shame her parents, but Tiyan was convinced it was not on such a grand scale. Knowing Eki as she did, she probably hadn't considered the consequences of her actions, including the possibility that no Benin man would marry an Alile woman.

Tiyan sighed. In her characteristic manner, Eki had retired to her bedroom, utterly unbothered by the mess she'd made. But somebody had to clean it up. Eki constantly required cleaning up after. Aiai refused to do it. Aiai requested that Eki take responsibility and clean up the mess herself. Eki's reputation suggested the mess wouldn't be cleaned. The matter would escalate. And when it did, it would affect the whole family. Not just Eki. So, someone else would have to get their hands dirty and clean it up.

This time, the buck stopped with her, Tiyan. She would discuss this with Usi tonight. Usi could make things right and save their family from scandal. Tiyan was uncertain about how far tradition would permit his intervention, but she was certain he would take action. She had complete faith in his ability to solve this issue.

There was a knock on her door so soft that she almost missed it.

"Come in," she called, smiling as her uncle, Chief Zogie Alile, entered her bedroom. She loved this man very much. He had saved her life. At thirteen, with no father, mother, or sibling, he had opened his arms and home to her. He had become her father, his wife, Aunt Ayi, had become her mother, and his daughters, Aisosa, Eseosa, and Eki, had become her siblings.

"Good evening, Uncle Zogie."

He cast her a swift, approving glance and smiled, then sat at the edge of the bed near her vanity stool.

"Tiyan, *ko'yọ*. Good evening. I see you are ready for your date with Chief Isekhure."

Tiyan frowned and shifted her gaze from the mirror to her uncle. "You're aware I am seeing Usi tonight?"

His smile conveyed both his awareness and approval. "I

am aware. Chief Isekhure is a very responsible young man. He won't take you out without telling me. He wished for me to be aware that his intentions were honourable. Not that I had any doubt. He is indeed a responsible young man, as I mentioned."

"Yes. I think so, too."

There was a pause as her uncle carefully considered what he was about to say next. "I saw Ekpen Orobator earlier today. He hinted at marriage."

"He did what?" Tiyan was furious. Was the man insane? He was fifteen years older than her twenty-four years and married with three children! Besides, he was the louse who had touched her inappropriately years ago.

Her uncle held up his hand. "Be assured, it will only happen over my dead body that he marries you."

Tiyan's face lit up with a smile; she was confident that her uncle always considered her best interests.

"He didn't come out expressly to say it; he was going around in circles, saying many things and saying nothing. But I am not a small child. I didn't respond because he hadn't said anything. I thought I should inform you that he may be a potential suitor. But Chief Isekhure would be a perfect match for you." Her uncle paused. "What do you think of him?"

Tiyan shrugged and pulled a face. It seemed a little odd to

be having this conversation with her uncle. "I think he's handsome and brilliant. And he's done well for himself. He's not blown his father's money but has built on the wealth. That's admirable."

Her uncle nodded silently. "So, you like him?"

Tiyan nodded. "I do. Very much."

"Okay." Her uncle sounded quite pleased. "He has my permission to woo you. I have no fear that he will act in an untoward manner. So, if you go out tonight, and you think that it's late and you can't come back, it's okay for you to return home in the morning."

As he rose to leave her bedroom, Tiyan watched him with a cheeky smile playing on her lips. "Is it okay to move in with him?" she teased.

He said nothing in response, but his don't-you-dare look had her in stitches as he left her room, shutting the door behind him.

Her phone vibrated. She picked it up. It was a text message from Usi.

I am on my way to you.

She smiled and texted back.

I am ready and waiting.

Shortly after, another text arrived.

Are you wearing something nice for me?

She laughed and texted.

That's for me to know and for you to find out. And stop texting while you're driving.

A few seconds later, his text came through.

Yes, Mother. LOL.

As Tiyan put the phone down, it rang. It was Mr Orobator. She shook her head and declined the call. The louse. He would not ruin her mood for the evening.

CHAPTER FOUR

As Usi brought his blue Range Rover Sport to a halt in front of the small grey and white detached duplex that was Chief Alile's residence, he was the happiest he had been in months. He exited his vehicle as Tiyan stepped through the single steel pedestrian gate.

"Hi." That was all he could muster as he gazed at her. She looked exquisite in her black halter-neck dress with an A-line skirt and an open slit in the middle that showed her pale, gorgeous legs as she walked. Strappy black stilettos made her legs appear even longer. Her hair, styled in the traditional *okuku* hairstyle earlier today, was in a ponytail falling past her shoulders.

"Hi," she responded, smiling at him and twirling. "You like?"

"I like. Very much," he assured her. *Probably too much*, he thought as he took her hand and ushered her into the front passenger seat. He put on her seat belt, his eyes catching a glimpse of her beautiful thighs revealed through the parting of her slit. He stepped back quickly, shut the door, and got behind the wheel.

"You don't mind having dinner with me in my house, do you?" he asked as he put on his seat belt and started the engine.

"Not at all. It sounds good."

"I planned to take you to dinner, but it's not appropriate for me to be seen wining and dining in public while the kingdom mourns. Please forgive me."

"There's nothing to forgive. I understand your position; besides, my mood tonight prefers a home-cooked meal to eating out." Tiyan assured him. "And it will be great to see inside your famous white house at last."

Usi chuckled. His house fascinated many, not only because of its size in the upscale part of the city, or its location on a mountaintop with vast land, but also because of its white interior and exterior. He loved white. His father had favoured white and said it was a symbol of purity and synonymous with the office of a chief priest. In designing his house, he had taken white to a new level. Thus, his abode became known as Isekhure White House among the kingdom's inhabitants, especially those who lived in the city.

"It will be my joy to show you around," he said.

She beamed him. "I will look forward to it."

As he drove through the electronically controlled gate and past the car parks on the left and right sides of the winding, sloping road, the sprawling twelve-bedroom mansion, set over three floors, came into view.

"Wow!" Tiyan exclaimed in delight, leaning forward and looking around her. "It's beautiful!"

"I'm glad you think so," he said.

It was his home, and he had driven through the main gate countless times, but he tried to picture what a first-time visitor might see: garden lamps and palm trees lined the sloping path up to the front entrance, with its imposing glass double doors and water fountain which was always a delight to guests.

He stopped the vehicle in front of the impressive doors, exited, and circled around to assist Tiyan from the front seat. While helping her, he threw his key to a driver who suddenly appeared and stood by him, ready to park the car.

"*Uruese.* Thank you," he said and turned to Tiyan. "We'll have dinner first because I'm famished, and then I'll show you around the house. The servant's quarters behind are as big as the main house, so my staff live there."

"It's a lovely, beautiful place to live," she said as he put his arm around her waist and led her through the double doors.

They entered the massive foyer with its white walls and marble floor. Large crystal chandeliers descended from the high ceiling, and in the centre stood a life-size bronze sculpture of a man in traditional attire holding the *Eben* royal sceptre. The hall was more than double the size of the ground floor of her uncle's house. Indeed, she estimated that the space was large enough to accommodate all the rooms of her uncle's house.

Usi paused as Tiyan stopped and looked around before letting her gaze fall on the statue. "Incredible," she muttered breathlessly. "Who is he?"

Usi looked at the statue with pride and then at Tiyan. "An ancestor of mine. He was also a chief priest. Let's eat, and then I'll show you around."

"This is delicious," Tiyan said as they ate the rich meal of fish stew, boiled rice with fried cubed plantains, and moin-moin, which was the main course. The starter had been a spicy ox-tail pepper soup.

Usi nodded in agreement. "Mrs Agbi is the best," he confirmed. "She has been with me since I returned from the US. She worked for my father before then. I coveted her. My mother is still unhappy, but I need her services more. She is an excellent housekeeper and cook." He put his cutlery down and picked up his glass of water.

"What was it like returning from the US to serve as chief priest in your father's stead?" Tiyan asked.

Usi shrugged. "I always knew I would be chief priest someday. I was born for it and groomed for it. Communing with gods was innate and part of my life from a child. I wished my father lived longer, solely because he was my father, not because I was captivated by Western life and reluctant to return home for my purpose."

Tiyan took a sip of her cranberry juice. "So, I guess there's no need to ask if you love being chief priest."

"No, there's no need to ask." He leaned back in his seat and spread his arms out wide. "Look at me. What else would I be if not chief priest of this kingdom?"

Tiyan glanced at him, clad in his jeans and polo shirt, and couldn't help but laugh. "As you are currently dressed, you don't resemble the chief priest of this kingdom."

"How about earlier today when you saw me at the Edaiken Palace?" he asked.

Tiyan frowned slightly as she tried to recall what he'd looked like in the traditional attire he had been wearing earlier that day.

"Come on." Usi sounded wounded. "It's only been a few hours. Don't tell me you've forgotten what I looked like. You are breaking my heart, T."

The door of the large dining room opened, and a smallish-looking elderly woman wearing a white apron over her Ankara midi dress entered, bearing a tray with dishes containing something that smelt divine.

“Ah, dessert is here.” Usi sat upright in his chair while Mrs. Agbi placed the tray at the centre of the table.

“Thank you, Mrs Agbi,” Tiyan said as the older woman turned to leave. She smiled in response and quietly retreated. Tiyan eyed the contents of the tray. There was a fruit salad platter, a platter of groundnut cake, and coconut candy. The feast, fit for a king, made Tiyan salivate.

"I told you she's the best," Usi said, amused.

“She’s going to blow my diet. But I don’t care. I am having a bit of everything.”

Usi chuckled as he leaned in to heap a plate with groundnut cake and coconut candy before passing it to her. “That’s what I like to hear.”

Tiyan took a bite of the coconut candy, and as it melted in her mouth, she shut her eyes. “Mmm. This is to die for.”

Usi grinned. “I like women who have a healthy appetite,” he said as he helped himself to some fruit salad. “I thought you might be one of those women constantly starving themselves to stay thin.”

“Oh no. Not me. I’m a person who lives to eat, hence the need for a diet and exercise.” She took another bite of the coconut candy. “I can see why you coveted Mrs Agbi and why your mum is upset. If I had a fabulous cook, and you stole her, we would have a problem."

Usi chuckled. "Do you cook?"

"I do. I cook well, but Mrs Agbi is on another level."

"I'd like to eat something you cook someday."

"It's a deal," Tiyan said. "But after all these delicious meals you've been spoiled with, you may throw mine in the bin."

Usi roared with laughter, and Tiyan joined him. As the laughter subsided and they ate their desserts, Tiyan remembered the issue troubling her. It was time to tell him about Eki's plight. If it could be called that. Eki was probably fast asleep now and not bothered about what tomorrow held.

"I need to tell you something," she began. "Can I trust you?"

Usi raised his head and leaned closer to communicate that she had his full attention. His eyebrows furrowed into a frown. "You can trust me. If we have a future together, I would prefer you approach me first with any issues." His frown deepened. "Does this relate to your uncle and his family? Are they bothering you?"

Tiyan hesitated. "It relates to my uncle and his family, but they are not bothering me. This affects them and also affects me because I am Alile."

He reached for his glass of water without taking his eyes off her. "Tell me," he encouraged.

Where did she start from? She wasn't one who drank; apparently, neither was Usi, for there was no alcohol on the table. She felt like she needed to drink something for a bit of courage.

"Eki has been chosen to be queen," she blurted out and belatedly realised how stupid she must sound. Of course, Usi would be aware of that.

He smiled, revealing that he was aware of the development. "It is as it should be. Is this what is bothering you?" Without waiting for her answer, he added, "It is her destiny."

Tiyan rubbed her temple before reaching for her glass of cranberry juice with an unsteady hand. Usi watched her like he was trying to read her mind. She took a sip and put her glass down.

"She has a virginity test tomorrow morning," she informed him.

Usi nodded to show this was not news to him. "And?"

"And she won't pass the test."

Usi turned to stone right before Tiyan's eyes. "Start from the beginning, and don't omit anything." His voice cut through the air like ice, chilling her to the bone, while his piercing gaze seemed to bore into her soul.

Tiyan nodded, feeling uneasy. "We travelled on holiday to Dubai, Paris and London," she began in a shaky voice.

"I am aware of this trip."

"Before we left, we discovered Eseosa, Eki's immediate older sister, was pregnant by Odaro, Eki's ex-boyfriend. My aunt played a major role in getting both together while Eki was in the UK studying towards her master's. Feeling angry and betrayed, Eki did something stupid to bring shame to the family. To her parents. During our vacation in London, she slept with a man named Owen Morgan at The Dorchester."

"Osad?" Usi asked, recognising Osad's alias.

Tiyan nodded as she licked her lips. "She was unaware of his identity. She only found out today. He's unaware of her true identity due to her clever makeup disguise. So, you see, if she fails the test, he won't believe she was the woman in his hotel room in London. No one will believe her, and our family will face complete ruin."

Usi stood and walked around the large, immaculate dining room, pausing occasionally in front of the continuous floor-to-ceiling window to gaze upon the vast ornamental garden beyond. From all indications, his appetite had disappeared. Well, so had hers, Tiyan thought. Just talking about what had happened made her realise how serious it was. If Usi failed to resolve this situation, the Alile family, not just Eki, was doomed.

"So, what you're trying to tell me is that Osad has already taken his wife's virginity, except, instead of doing it the traditional way, he's done it in a hotel room?"

"Yes," Tiyan replied. "She hasn't been with anyone else."

"Of course, she hasn't! Otherwise, she would be dead!" He turned to look at Tiyan. "Do you realise the seriousness of what she did? Does your cousin have a death wish? The gods chose her for Osad. If she had given her virginity to another man, she would have died! If he hailed from Benin, he would have died!"

Tiyan instinctively raised both hands to her mouth, her eyes wide with disbelief as she struggled to process what she had just heard.

"Do you think it's a game when the gods select a wife for the future king of the Benin Kingdom?" He didn't wait for a response. "It seems that you and your cousin may not be fully aware of the tradition. Fortunately for her, she ended up in Osad's bed."

"Yes," Tiyan replied softly.

"And as for Osad. What did he think he was doing?" Usi appeared to be talking to no one, so Tiyan watched him silently. "Osad has taken his wife's virginity in some hotel?" he asked no one and scratched his head. "Osad, you will be the death of me."

"What are you going to do now?" Tiyan asked.

He looked at her as if he had just realised he wasn't by himself. "The unfortunate event should not have occurred, so I must seek guidance from the gods tonight for a resolution."

Tiyan looked downcast. He walked to her, pulled her out of her chair, and held her chin, forcing her to look up at him.

"It will be okay. I will get Eki where she needs to be without exposing her. Do you trust me?"

Tiyan nodded. "Yes, I trust you."

"Good. Then leave it with me. I will take care of everything."

As his head lowered and their lips connected, Tiyan's body ignited like in her dream. His powerful arms enveloped her in a warm and secure embrace, filling her with an overwhelming happiness that radiated from within. She belonged in his embrace. This man would take care of her. She had not a single doubt. He would do anything and everything to protect Eki and the Alile family for her sake. She let go of her fears and relaxed in his arms, permitting herself to enjoy his kiss.

CHAPTER FIVE

Once she had got Eki's story off her chest, Tiyan relaxed in Usi's company. After dinner, he showed her around his massive and exquisitely furnished home. The mansion sat on five acres of land. It boasted twelve bedrooms, an indoor swimming pool, a state-of-the-art gym, a cinema, and reception rooms of various sizes.

A sports dome with lawn tennis, volleyball, and basketball courts sat on the vast land that separated the main building from the servant's quarters. After the tour, they retired to the recreation room with their drinks. Just like the other rooms she had seen, this room was all white with white furnishings. It doubled as a library with floating wall-to-wall shelves filled with books. A pool table stood in the room's centre, while Tiyan noticed small board games on side tables.

"My office as chief priest means I socialise very little in public. So, I have ensured my home has all the entertainment I need. But if you like to go out, we can travel for extended weekend breaks once the coronation is over. I am more relaxed outside Benin."

Tiyan stood in front of the white shelf that spanned an entire wall, gently running a hand over the spines of books dedicated to the history of ancient Benin. And then, she turned towards him. "I am good either way. Dressing up and going out or snuggling on the couch in sweats both work for me."

"You are perfect for me." His gaze shifted from the pool table to Tiyan. "Do you play?"

"If by 'play' you mean, do I understand how to use the long stick to shove the balls so they roll into the holes on the table, then yes, I play."

Usi set his glass of sparkling grape juice on the pool table, shaking with laughter. Tiyan joined in the mirth.

"Even your terminology tells me you don't play."

Tiyan shrugged and sipped her cranberry juice. "It's a silly game to me. It's like football, where twenty-two people chase a ball, and I'm unsure why. But I'll play if you want."

"You're a good sport. I like that."

"Anything to alleviate the chief priest's boredom."

Usi bowed slightly. "Madam, the kingdom is in your debt."

Tiyan giggled and put down her drink as Usi passed her a cue. "This long stick is called a cue. First rule: Get acquainted with the equipment."

"Yes, sir." Tiyan looked at the cue in her hand. "This is going to be such fun."

"That's the general idea," Usi said as he arranged the pool balls in a rack. "I love games, pool, monopoly, chess; you name it. It's one way I relax. My father was the same too. Whenever he was in the US, we would play for hours, sometimes into the early morning hours. It was a wonderful bonding experience. His time to teach me life lessons."

"You must miss him a lot."

Usi looked up from arranging the balls. "I do," he admitted. "I don't mention it to others because they don't see me as a man but a celestial being without emotions."

"Does that bother you?"

Usi frowned as he removed the rack from the neatly arranged pool balls. "Yes and no," he said. "It helps because I am not taken for granted. But, it means I present a side that isn't always the side I want people to see."

"Sounds tough," Tiyan murmured, leaning over the billiard table to take a shot. "I am curious. What exactly do you do as chief priest? I have a bit of understanding, but I'm eager to hear your perspective."

Usi moved closer to her and put an arm around her waist so his right hand lay over her hand, holding the end of the cue. He loosened her grip so it was relaxed but controlled. Then, he slid the cue between her index and middle fingers with his left hand. Tiyan angled her head to look at him, and their eyes met and held.

"My main duty is to pray for the Oba." He released her and stepped back. "That's how you hold the cue."

"Thank you," Tiyan muttered and hit the cue ball. The balls broke up in different directions but failed to enter the pockets. "How lame." She straightened and grinned at Usi.

"Not bad for a first attempt." He grinned and moved to take his place at the table, sipping his drink as he did.

"So you pray for the Oba, and that's it?"

"Of course not. That's the primary duty. I am the king's priest, praying for the king and leading other priests in doing the same. I am also his advisor and hold the fort for him on all spiritual matters. Moreover, I tend to the royal ancestors and perform all royal rites on behalf of the king."

"Oh. That's huge."

"It's a great responsibility. And a lot deeper than what I have shared." Usi picked a cue and leaned forward over the table, his eye on the target ball.

"So, of all the different things you do, which brings you the greatest fulfilment?"

"Sounds like I am on Oprah." He shook with laughter.

"Well, you wanted to get acquainted, so answer the question," she said.

Usi smiled. "I think settling community and land disputes is where I find the greatest fulfilment." He straightened, moved slightly to his left, and leaned over the table again. "It's not what most people want to hear, but it's the truth." He hit the balls and straightened, watching delightedly as they fell into several pockets.

"Show off," Tiyan said, pursed her lips, and caused Usi to roar with laughter.

They played and chatted for close to an hour. Usi asked about her life with her uncle and aunt and was curious about her dreams and aspirations. She found it easy to talk to him and answered his questions more willingly than she had with Alexander.

She reversed the situation, temporarily putting him on the spot. She inquired about his life in America and what else he did besides being a chief priest. He was still a stock market trader with a vast portfolio of companies across America, Europe, and Africa, in which he owned large shares.

They lost track of time as they chatted, and when it was midnight, he looked at his watch triumphantly.

"It's too late for you to leave now," he announced.

Tiyan shook her head. "Like you believed I was still planning to leave."

He chuckled as he took her by the hand and pulled her to her feet. "I will show you to your room."

Hand in hand, they walked up the staircase and down the main second-floor corridor, finally arriving at a room. He had called it the princess bedroom while taking her around the house. As he opened the door, he looked at her.

"I requested my driver to collect a few of your belongings."

Tiyan arched an eyebrow upon realising her small overnight case was in the bedroom. "Seriously?" she inquired. "You take a lot of liberties. Who packed my case?"

He shrugged. "I think your aunt did, but I'm not sure. I told your uncle you weren't returning home and needed a few things. He said he would ask your aunt to arrange something. My driver drove over and collected the bag."

"Why didn't you just ask me to pack a bag when I was coming?"

He angled his head to look at her. "Would you have agreed?"

"No," she said.

He shrugged again. "And that's why I didn't ask you."

"What's the need for me to spend the night?"

"Because you are my wife, and this is your home." He spoke like the answer should have been obvious to her. "I would marry you today, but your uncle has other ideas. I am happy to let him have his way on when the bride price is paid, provided he doesn't keep me waiting too long. However, I don't want to be apart from you in the meantime. I want to see you at mealtimes and come home knowing you are waiting for me."

"This is weird. I wished for a marriage proposal before marriage. I expected to be wooed, not whisked off to some castle and locked up."

Usi smiled. "All in good time. Miss Alile. All in good time," he assured. "You will be wooed, and there will be a marriage proposal that will leave you enchanted."

"After I move in." Tiyan pointed out.

"Is that such a bad thing?" Usi asked. "People do it all the time."

"Well, I am certain my uncle will never let me move in with you."

"Don't be too sure," Usi said. "I have my way of getting what I want. But I'd rather spend my time and energy convincing you to move in."

Tiyan narrowed her eyes in deep contemplation, and Usi

kissed her forehead.

"Sleep well, my beloved. I have work to do."

"Does that work have any connection to fixing Eki's situation?" Tiyan asked.

He winked as he turned to leave. "You bet."

Crown Prince Osad Edoni would be the death of him!

It was Usi's conclusion as he sat on the floor in his shrine and communed with the gods, trying to figure out a way to handle what was a sacrilege. He knew what he had to do, what he must do. In the morning, he would go to the palace hospital and cancel the virginity test. It could not hold.

His interference would mean Osad was getting a wife who was not a virgin. That was unacceptable. But the same Osad had taken her virginity. Nonetheless, his interference could result in a backlash. But he was the chief priest. He would appease the gods. He would need to pacify the gods, anyway, seeing as Osad broke with tradition and took his wife's virginity in a hotel room in a foreign land.

The idea of telling Osad about Eki being the woman he slept with in London didn't come up. It would be easy to make a guess about Osad's reaction at this point, considering he wanted nothing to do with Alile's daughter. He would publicly shame her and cancel all plans for the wedding. Tiyan would be devastated. She had trusted him with this secret. He could not and would not betray her trust.

He would have to walk into the hospital tomorrow and cancel the virginity test. He had sufficient authority as chief priest to pull it off, and no one would challenge his authority. And then a thought entered his head. He would go in the company of Edosa Aihie. Edosa was another prominent chief, as he was not only Osad's best friend but also married to Osad's youngest sister, Orobosa.

Usi grinned and stroked his chin thoughtfully. Edosa wouldn't like being dragged into this But Usi trusted him to be discrete. And with Edosa by his side, no one would utter a word or bat an eyelid. Yes, that was what he would do. He would call Edosa early in the morning. Like him, Edosa was an early riser. No details would be shared over the phone; he would simply say an urgent assignment required Edosa's involvement, and he would come around to pick him up.

CHAPTER SIX

Tiyan slept badly. It had nothing to do with her being in a strange bed. The princess bedroom was beautiful, with a sitting area, bathroom, and dressing room. She adored it and could easily acclimate to the enormous bed, much larger than the one she had at home. Her lack of sleep stemmed from her conversation with Usi concerning Eki.

Had she done the right thing in telling Usi? She wondered.

He assured her of his trustworthiness, and she had faith in him, yet she couldn't help but ponder the consequences if she had misjudged and everything went wrong. Eki would kill her, and who could blame her? Her uncle and aunt would say she had destroyed the family. The thing she tried to prevent would occur, and it would be her fault. She worried continually, and after tossing and turning, she fell into a deep sleep, where everything she feared played out.

Usi's plan to help Eki backfired, and Eki was furious with her because, like a wildfire, the rumour of Eki being deflowered had spread around the kingdom. Her uncle and aunt were livid; they accused her of ruining their chances of being parents-in-law to the king. Eki's older sisters, Aiai and Eseosa, were there too, and they accused her of ruining Eki's life.

"Why did you say anything?" Eki yelled at her. "I trusted you, and you betrayed that trust!"

"I was only trying to help!" Tiyan tried to explain as she looked from Eki to Eki's parents and sisters. But no one was willing to listen.

"You are trouble, Tiyan!" they chorused.

Feeling a deep sense of rejection, Tiyan ran away. Her uncle's home was no longer conducive. The time had come to return home. At home, she would feel better. In a comforting embrace, her father would hold her and assure her everything would be all right. Recognising she had only intended to help her cousin, her mother would listen to her explanation. Her brother, Osamu, would make her laugh and bring back her happiness.

But when she got home, it was different. The house was unchanged, but her family was missing. She rang the doorbell, and Mr Orobator opened the door. His smile was so unsettling that it made her feel ill. He held out his arms to her.

"Come to me, Tiyan," he said.

She shook her head, stepping back slowly. Why was Mr Orobator in her family's home? Then she remembered the house was rented out to another family. Her family no longer lived there. Quickly, she revisited the accident—the final moments spent with her family.

Her dad was behind the wheel, and her mum was in the front passenger seat, smiling and telling a story, as was her custom when they travelled. She and her brother were in the backseat, trying to appear interested in their mother's story. Suddenly, she'd had a premonition of danger. She had seen nothing to make her feel that way. But she'd known that evil loomed.

"Dad, slow down!" she screamed. Then, everything went dark.

The dream quickly transitioned to the funeral day; as she walked slowly behind the three caskets, she screamed, fell to the ground and wailed.

"I want to die, too! I want to die, too!" Tiyan sobbed uncontrollably.

Suddenly, he was there, the man who'd kissed her senseless in her other dream. He was on the floor with her, holding her in a grip that was strong yet gentle. He comforted her like her father had done many times, murmuring in her ear as one did to a child.

"Wake up, T. It's only a dream."

Tiyan opened her eyes and realised he was right. It had been a dream. A horrific dream. Yes, her family was gone, but Eki and her family had not rejected her. Her eyelids were damp.

She had really been crying. It had all appeared so real.

"I had a bad dream about my family and the accident," she explained to Usi, who lay in her bed spooning with her. She experienced an unusual sense of solace from his presence and his arm that enveloped her.

"I heard you wailing," he said. "Do you usually have bad dreams about them and the accident?"

"Not so much these days. I haven't had a bad dream about the accident in years."

"Why tonight?"

Tiyan exhaled softly, adjusting her position to rest her head on his chest, nestled gently in the cradle of his arms.

"I had a dream where my uncle and his family turned me away, and I returned home, except I had no home, and the dream continued to the accident." Tears filled her eyes.

Usi brushed away the tears with a thumb as they rolled down her cheeks. "Why would your uncle and his family reject you? Is this something they've done before?"

Tiyan raised her head to look into his eyes. "No." She shook her head. Her uncle and his family had always treated her with love, acceptance, and kindness.

As Usi frowned, she decided it was time to explain. "I think my worries brought it on." She looked away.

Usi raised a brow. "Does this relate to me?" he asked. "If it is about you being here, I have made my intentions known to your uncle, and he knows I am a man of my word. Also, I would–"

Tiyan put a finger to his lips to silence him. "That's not what had me worried," she said. "I was worried because I had shared with you things about Eki that I shouldn't have, and although I did it to save my family, if it backfires, I fear the same family will reject me."

Usi grabbed her shoulder and shook her slightly, forcing her to look at him. "You must trust me. I will let nothing bad happen to you or your family. I will do everything I can to protect you and the Alile name."

He would. She saw it in his eyes. "Thank you."

"For nothing." He pulled her closer and kissed her forehead.

She rested her head on his chest, feeling his arms encircle her. It was an unparalleled feeling. This man meant every word he said.

"The gods preserved you for me, T. Never say you want to die again. No matter what happens, you are mine now, and wherever I am is home." He tightened his grip. "I want you to forget the past and live for me."

Tiyan closed her eyes as she breathed in the faint scent of

his cologne. "I will live for you," she promised. "No matter what happens, I am yours now, and wherever you are is home."

"Good girl," he praised.

She smiled. Usi Isekhure was everything she had prayed for. He was perfect for her.

"Tell me about your parents and brother. I want to learn about them and your life before the accident."

She lay on her side, propping her head with a pillow, allowing her to look into his eyes as she spoke. "My dad was an engineer, and my mum owned the bakery next door. The houses are semi-detached bungalows belonging to my parents. We lived in one, and my mother ran her bakery from the other. She baked and sold bread and delicious pastries. Osamu, my brother, was two years my senior, and after school, we would spend time with my mum in the bakery. We claimed to help, but just wanted to eat the baked goods straight from the oven. The staff were friendly and humoured us. I remember the bakers teaching us to mould the bread dough and to stuff meat pies. Next, we'd go for after-school lessons nearby, riding our bikes and shouting at one another to slow down. When we returned home, Mum would have closed from the bakery for the day and would be home making dinner.

"Dad would be home after we freshened up. We would have dinner as a family and talk about our day. Dad would tell funny stories and make us all laugh. Osamu was a lot like him. He used to tell a lot of funny stories, too. They both made Mum and me laugh a lot. We were a happy family. Osamu aspired to be an engineer like Dad, while I aimed to become an accountant. Mum said I would join her in business when I left school and run the business and admin side of things while she focused on baking."

"What happened to the bakery and house?"

"My uncle needed money to care for me, so he rented them out." Tiyan sighed wistfully. "I miss my old life."

Usi pulled her into his arms and held her tighter. Tiyan knew he'd go to any lengths to make her happy, to alleviate her pain. With a man like Usi, she could move into the future and create a happy family.

"How are you here, anyway? How did you get in?" She looked toward the room door. "I am certain I locked it."

Usi looked at the door and shrugged. "I'm sure you did, and it should still be locked. I didn't touch it."

Tiyan gazed at him, shocked. "Then how did you -?"

"A secret door lies within your dressing room. It connects your room to mine. I was in my shrine, next door, so it was easy to hear you sob."

"Oh," Tiyan responded, suddenly feeling silly.

"How did you think I got in?"

She drew circles on his pyjama top with her finger, not wanting to look at him. "Well, I thought that…" she shrugged, unwilling to complete her sentence.

"You thought that as chief priest, I walked in through the wall?" He erupted into laughter, and Tiyan jabbed him in the ribs. "I suppose I can do it, but why would I want to when I can just walk through a door?"

Tiyan couldn't help but burst into laughter. "Okay. I admit, that was a ludicrous thought."

"Seeing you laugh is delightful." He cradled her face. "Your weeping drove a dagger through my heart. I left my shrine vowing to kill anyone who had caused you such distress. But there was no one. It was you getting yourself agitated."

"I was worried sick," Tiyan confessed. "It was a while before I fell asleep."

"But last night, when we talked about this, you said you trusted me. Invariably, you lied." He sounded displeased.

Tiyan refuted his claim. "I do trust you. I kept imagining countless things that could go wrong, things beyond your control."

"Nothing is out of my control. Not concerning this issue. Now go to sleep, little lady." With a firm hand, he guided her head back to its position on his chest.

"You didn't show me your shrine when you took me on a tour around the house," Tiyan accused, pouting.

Usi sighed. "I can see the sleep's gone." He put some space between them and climbed out of the bed.

Tiyan feared that she had offended him. His shrine was probably off-limits to anyone and everyone. As she opened her mouth to apologise, he held out his hand.

"Come along, then," he urged her. "You can see the shrine and my bedroom suite."

Excitedly, she jumped out of bed and threw her silk dressing gown over her nightdress. She placed her hand in his, and he walked towards the secret door in her dressing room. As they neared the door, he stopped and glanced back.

"It's not your time, is it?" he asked.

For a moment, Tiyan was confused. Her subtle frown likely revealed it.

"You can't enter my bedroom or the shrine when it's your time. Is it?" he asked again.

"No. No, it isn't," she hurriedly denied. "I was just a little surprised. Never has any man asked me something so personal."

"I am your husband, and you need to learn the protocol

for being the chief priest's wife."

Discerning his seriousness, she nodded in agreement.

"Good," he affirmed. "Rule number one. Never come to my suite of rooms when it is your time. Understood?"

Tiyan nodded. "Understood."

"Rule number two is an extension of rule number one: during your time, refrain from cooking for me, eating together, sharing a bed, or travelling in the same vehicle."

Tiyan nodded, her eyes widening. It sounded like there were many rules to remember and abide by.

"My mother and Mrs Agbi will teach you many other rules. Certain instructions will be simple to follow, while others may prove more challenging. But remember, this is your destiny. This is what you were born for and the reason the gods preserved you."

He turned, pushed open the door, and led her into a lobby. It seemed like a different house. There were rooms on the left and right and a door straight ahead.

"That's my private sitting room," he informed her as he followed her eyes to the great oak door. "My bedroom is left, the dining room is right, my shrine is here, and right opposite is my home office."

He walked into the shrine, his hand firmly locked in hers.

He looked at her while she took in the room with amazement.

What was she thinking? He wondered. *Was it too much for her? Was he exposing too much too soon?*

Tiyan looked around her. As a Benin woman, she took pride in her knowledge of her people's culture and tradition. However, this was a completely new experience for her. Although it wasn't the official shrine, its beauty profoundly reflected the essence of the Benin people, their culture, and traditions.

There were countless bronze sculptures depicting the gods of the land, and the *Ada and Eben* royal sceptres hung in a place of authority. The walls were white, and the curtains were red. There were calabashes of various shapes and sizes, empty calabashes, calabashes with cowries, calabashes with native chalk and calabashes with kola nuts. And on the floor, an array of gin bottles, surely for libation to the gods. Against one wall leaned a heavy iron rod.

"What's that?" Tiyan pointed to the staff against the wall.

Usi's eyes followed the direction of her hand and gaze. "That's the *ukhurhe*. The ancestral staff. I use it when I pray for the king."

Tiyan nodded speechlessly. "Thank you for letting me see it." She looked at Usi, whose eyes were watching her intently.

"It's remarkable."

"Thank you. I think so, too." He looked over the room. "I had it created when I built the house. It is a replica of the main shrine and everything I dreamed it would be. I spend a lot of time here."

"I can see why," she said.

He led her away and showed her the rest of the suite. "Are you happy now?" he asked as the tour ended.

"Yes," she said as he led her back to her bedroom. "Why didn't you show it to me before?"

"I didn't want to reveal my life too soon and overwhelm you." He frowned. "My life is not as colourful internally as it appears externally. Assuming the role of chief priest comes at a price; few women can marry a man called to a life of duty and sacrifice."

In his eyes, she saw his doubt. She smiled and moved into his arms. "But if I was born for this and preserved for this, then surely I can?" She wrapped her arms around his neck and stood on tiptoe to kiss him.

When she arose the following morning, he was gone. She couldn't remember when he departed. It must have been very early. After the tour, he'd taken her back to her bedroom and stayed with her. She'd been exhausted, and feeling secure in his arms, she had slept when her head touched his chest. She frowned as she realised what time it was. A note was left on the pillow he slept on. She opened it.

T,

You were sleeping so soundly I couldn't bear to wake you. I have gone to take care of the issue with Eki. Mrs Agbi has breakfast ready for you, so eat before you leave. A car and driver are available for you.

See you tonight.

Usi

CHAPTER SEVEN

"Do you mind telling me what is going on?" Edosa Aihie asked as he climbed into the front passenger seat of Usi's Range Rover.

"You're accompanying me to the palace," Usi said.

Engaging his reverse gear, he departed from the driveway of Emotan, a semi-detached duplex featuring earthen walls, a pristine front garden, and a statue of Queen Idia. It was one of several buildings in the Royal Palace of the Queen Mother and where Edosa and his wife, Orobosa were lodged for their stay in Benin and the forthcoming coronation ceremony.

Edosa turned to face him, while putting on his seatbelt. "You already said so on the phone." He sounded irritated. "Why are we going to the palace? What's happening there? Osad is at the Edaiken Palace."

"Yes. But we need to go to the palace hospital to stop the virginity test."

Edosa looked at him as if he had grown two heads. Usi kept his eyes on the road as he exited through the monumental bronze gates of the palace and navigated his vehicle through the morning traffic in the busy city.

"Usi, what is our business with a virginity test?" Edosa

asked.

"The girl Osad has chosen to marry, Chief Alile's daughter, is not a virgin."

Edosa appeared surprised by this piece of news. "The same girl you and your father said the gods chose to be queen? She is not a virgin?"

Usi shook his head. "She isn't."

"So, how is that our business? If she is not a virgin, then he won't marry her. It's that simple!"

Again, Usi shook his head. "It's not that simple!" he stated. "She was handpicked for Osad by the gods."

Edosa shrugged. "Osad never desired her, so her loss of virginity resolves everything. We should mind our business."

"We are going to stop the virginity test. Osad will remain unaware and proceed with the marriage." Usi kept his voice calm as he waited for Edosa's outburst.

"Are you mad?" Edosa asked, raising his voice. "Are you planning to trick the king into marrying a non-virgin? Do you want to die? Well, if you do, I don't. I am not doing this. You have gone mad!"

"Edosa, calm down and hear me out." Usi guided his vehicle from the bustling street onto the quieter, lengthy road leading to the Royal Palace of the Oba of Benin.

"Hear you out? *Uzuọ a!* You are stupid, and you are talking nonsense. Are you forgetting who Osad is? He is the Oba of Benin. He is deity number four hundred and one in this kingdom. Do you think we are talking about a man we grew up with? He is Oba!"

Usi took his eyes off the road momentarily to glance at Edosa. "Technically, he is not yet Oba. The coronation ceremony has not happened. He has not undergone the traditional rites that make him a deity."

Edosa was far from convinced. "So, what? It is safe to deceive him? You are talking rubbish. I want no part in this. Let the lady marry the man who deflowered her."

Usi sighed and shook his head; Edosa's reaction was exactly as he had anticipated. "Think about this for a minute. What do you think would have happened to the man who took her virginity?"

Edosa shrugged. "He is probably dead. And she should be dead too."

"She should be. And why isn't she?"

Edosa slammed his hand on the dashboard. "Enough of the stupid questions. I am not in the mood. If you have something to say, say it!"

"Owen Morgan deflowered her. In London. Four days

ago."

Now, he had Edosa's attention. "Osad?!"

Usi nodded. "He doesn't recognise her. Don't ask me why. Something to do with a makeup disguise."

"But she knows him, which is probably why she stuttered when she saw him yesterday. The poor thing."

"I missed most of it because my attention was on Tiyan."

"That much was obvious," Edosa said drily. "But if she knows it's Osad, why doesn't she tell him, or why don't you tell him? Why play this stupid game that could get us both killed?"

"Osad has always resented that he was destined to marry Chief Alile's daughter. If he knows she came to him in The Dorchester, he will brand her a whore and call off the wedding."

Edosa shrugged nonchalantly. "And so?"

"That will destroy the Alile family. I can't let that happen. Not when my future wife is Alile."

Edosa let out a dry, humourless laugh, the sound echoing with a hint of frustration. "So, you're playing this dangerous game to rescue your future in-laws? And you drag me into it so I can die beside you for nothing?!"

"Relax!" Usi tried to calm him. "Nobody is going to die. I am the chief priest, remember? I am aware of the methods to appease the gods."

Edosa glanced out the window as they drove through the palace gates. "Well, I hope that includes Osad because he will be one angry deity when he finds out what we've done."

Upon their arrival at the hospital, a nurse informed them that Eki had already arrived and was waiting to see the doctor. They proceeded directly to the doctor's office. Wearing a revered chief priest's face, Usi informed the doctor about the gods' prohibition of the examination.

"The gods handpicked Eki Aile to marry Crown Prince Osad Edoni. Examining her implies the gods chose an impure woman for the king. Their wrath is about to be incurred; therefore, the virginity test will not hold," he informed a bemused Dr Idah. "Unless you are suggesting the gods have chosen a non-virgin as the future queen of Benin."

"*Ého*! The gods forbid, Chief Isekhure, no such thought crossed my mind," Dr Idah denied, rising to her feet and shaking her head vehemently.

"Good." Usi left the office abruptly, with Edosa close behind.

While departing, they unexpectedly crossed paths with Eki, who seemed just as bewildered as the doctor upon learning of the virginity test being cancelled. Usi chose not to repeat the lie he told the doctor.

"We're good," he said instead as he left the hospital with Edosa.

"You lied through your straight white teeth!" Edosa said, climbing into Usi's vehicle.

"It was necessary." Usi started the vehicle and drove out of the hospital's car park.

"You lied against the gods," Edosa said. "They are going to kill us, make us mad, or turn us into lepers. Or perhaps mad lepers."

Usi might have laughed if the situation hadn't been so serious. "Cease your worries. We have taken the necessary actions. I will appease the gods, and everything will be fine. Trust me."

As Usi said the words, his heart sank. He had never uttered a word that the gods had not put in his mouth. His father raised him to understand the weight his words carried, and from a child, he had chosen his words carefully. Falsely attributing words to the gods was never his way. He had never done it till today. But it had to be done. He could not allow Eki to be shamed in the hospital when the doctor discovered she was no virgin and picked up the phone to convey the message to Osad.

Osad's dislike for Eki persisted. Usi knew this. His

decision to marry her had nothing to do with his wanting her, and it certainly had nothing to do with the prophecy. Osad was fulfilling an agenda of his own, but in time, he would realise the hands of fate had guided him into destiny.

"Osad will find out about this; you realise that, don't you?"

Edosa's question caused Usi to snap out of his reverie, and he shrugged. Osad would find out and was more likely to find out from Eki. But he sensed it would not happen right away, and it would not matter when it did. Osad might strike him in the face, just like in the past when Usi provoked him, but it wouldn't go beyond that.

"Eki will tell him about what we've done, but it won't matter too much."

Edosa looked at him sceptically. "For your sake, I certainly hope so."

When Tiyan arrived home, Eki was out. She would be at the palace hospital undergoing the virginity test. Her heart began to beat slightly quicker.

How did Usi plan to resolve the situation?

He had not shared his plans with her, no doubt wanting her to trust him without telling her how he planned to rectify the situation. She sighed. Details were unnecessary for her. His early departure for the palace to resolve the matter sufficed.

She was in her bedroom, attempting to rest after a night of little sleep when her phone beeped. She perceived it was a text from Usi, and sure enough, it was.

Done and dusted.

She smiled.

You are my superstar. What will I do without you?

A few seconds later, he responded.

I'd much rather consider what you can do with me.

She laughed.

See you tonight.

A few seconds later, his text came through.

I'm counting the hours.

As Tiyan set her phone down, she was overflowing with happiness. She was completely unaware of what Usi had done and how he had resolved the problem. And it didn't matter. Presently, her contentment lay in Usi's resolution of the problem.

Eki returned from her trip to the palace hospital and announced she had not taken a virginity test. She said Usi declared it was unnecessary. Tiyan vehemently denied any involvement, despite Eki's suspicion that she had something to do with it. Eki would not appreciate her telling her business to

Usi. So, she would be quiet about her involvement and hope that if Eki ever found out the truth, she would see that Tiyan had meant well.

She was elated as Usi's driver picked her up later. Sitting in the backseat of the white Mercedes Maybach, she reflected on what Usi had done. She understood the significant risk he took in making that decision. It could affect his relationship with the future Oba. It might even affect his liaison with the gods and his ability to be an effective mouthpiece.

She prayed he had not paid a price too high for her benefit. With nothing to offer except her hand in marriage, Tiyan decided to marry him if he still desired her. It was the least she could do. A man's sacrifice for a woman implied his seriousness in linking their family names. Usi's actions today made his intention to marry her clear. She intended to say yes when he proposed and, in the interim, build a solid relationship with him.

Her phone rang, and she pulled it out of her tote bag, looked at the screen, and sighed. Why wouldn't Mr Orobator leave her alone?

"Good evening, sir." Her voice was as cold as she intended it to be. She glanced at the driver, but he gave no sign he was listening in on her call. Not that she had anything to hide.

"Tiyan! My darling! You have been avoiding me. I learnt from your uncle that you have returned from your trip but have yet to visit me so we can talk. And you haven't been taking my calls. When are you coming over for a chat?"

"Mr Orobator, I don't think we have anything to discuss. As I told you before I travelled on holiday, I want the house and the bakery and will not sell. Inform me of the earliest possible time you can vacate both properties." She ended the call and held her breath while waiting for the text she was certain would follow.

Darling, stop being stubborn. You are a woman. What plans do you have for a house? You don't need landed property; you need a man to look after you and give you children. I blame your uncle, who gave you a say concerning the properties.

Tiyan glanced up from the screen to see the driver pulling up in front of the house. Usi stood in front of the glass doors—her very own superstar. She tossed the phone with its offensive message into her tote bag and climbed out of the car before the driver could help her.

She made a beeline for him and flung herself into his arms. He picked her up and twirled her around, his arms holding her tight.

As he set her down on her feet, Tiyan cradled his face. She looked at him in wonder as he kept his arms firmly wrapped around her waist. He was a man quite unlike any she had met. She would be eternally grateful to him and for him.

"My hero," she muttered, staring into his eyes dreamily.

"So, will you move in?" Usi asked before he kissed her.

"Maybe," she responded, giggling as he rolled his eyes in mock exasperation.

"We'll discuss that later. We must go now; my mother is expecting us for dinner."

Tiyan's eyes widened. "Your mother!"

"Yes, I have one. I believe I mentioned her last night. This chief priest didn't fall from the sky, as you might assume." He laughed at his joke, and Tiyan, joining in the mirth, playfully jabbed him in the ribs.

"I know you have a mother; I just didn't realise I would meet her today."

He shrugged. "The earlier, the better."

"I should probably get changed." Tiyan looked at her mini floral print dress.

Usi nodded to show his agreement. "I love the dress, but my mother is a very conservative Benin woman despite her years spent travelling the world."

Tiyan cringed in mock horror. "Say no more; I am off to get changed. Good thing I brought a few items with me."

"Glad to see you're following my advice and moving in."

"A few items for a day, or maybe two." Tiyan corrected him as she walked away.

CHAPTER EIGHT

Usi's father's house differed from his. The land was extensive, and the house was white. It was not a three-storey or two-storey but an endless bungalow with endless width and breadth.

The breathtaking landscape design combined well-cared-for carpet grass, white limestone gravel, and interlocking tiles. Red and purple bougainvillaea flowers adorned the white fence, and palm trees encircled the building and enhanced its beauty.

Tiyan was surprised to see her uncle's old Volvo parked in front of the house as they drove through the double wrought-iron gates opened by a uniformed guard. She looked at Usi and frowned.

"What is my uncle doing here?"

Usi brought his BMW X7 to a halt beside the other car. "It's not your uncle. When I called my mother to say we were on our way, she mentioned your aunt was visiting with her. I don't think she's staying for dinner, though. She's likely waiting because my mother must have told her we're coming."

"Interesting," Tiyan murmured as she climbed out of the vehicle.

Her aunt was notorious for meddling in the love lives of

her children, including Tiyan, a daughter of sorts. She was undoubtedly here to ensure the burgeoning relationship between Tiyan and Usi led to marriage.

Usi took her hand and approached the curtained triple-track sliding glass doors. A young girl, about thirteen years old, wearing denim dungarees, a T-shirt, and glasses, immediately opened the door. She grinned at Usi, revealing her braces.

"Good evening, Uncle Usi. Good evening, ma'am," she hurriedly greeted and pointed to a set of double bronze doors with the *Ada and Eben* royal sceptres. "Mum is in the main sitting room."

"Thank you, Ododo." Usi playfully tugged at her braids, causing peals of laughter to erupt from the teen.

As they walked through the foyer, resembling a museum due to a rich display of Benin bronze artefacts, Usi pulled Tiyan close and murmured, "Mrs Agbi's granddaughter. She lives with my mum."

"Oh," Tiyan said before Usi pushed the door open and ushered her into the large room with its white luxury sofas, white marble floor and gold curtains.

"Tiyan! *Woyeh*? How are you?" Mrs Alile enthusiastically greeted Tiyan as she entered the room hand in hand with Usi. She looked from one to the other, and her smile widened.

"Aunt Ayi, good evening." Tiyan tried to sound pleased, but inside, she thought, *Oh! Be gone already!*

Usi greeted Mrs Alile and his mother before leading Tiyan towards her for the formal introduction.

"Mum, this is Tiyan Alile, my future wife. Tiyan, this is my mother, Chief Mrs Isekhure."

Usi's mother was a plump, light-skinned woman gorgeously dressed in a white cotton lace maxi dress heavily embroidered around the neck and chest. Over her hair, she wore a head wrap made from the same fabric as her dress. On her neck, she wore beautiful white coral beads.

"Good evening, ma'am. It is a pleasure to meet you," Tiyan said, dropping low in curtsey.

Chief Mrs Isekhure rose and immediately pulled Tiyan to her feet and into a tight embrace.

"My darling, the pleasure is mine." Usi's mother pulled back and cradled Tiyan's face. "Usi has told me a lot about you. I am so sorry to hear about the passing of your parents and sibling. That experience must have been traumatic for you."

"Yes. But that was a long time ago," Mrs Alile said. "Tiyan has now become a woman and has surmounted the pain."

Other than a glance and polite smile in Mrs Alile's direction, Usi's mother did nothing else to acknowledge the statement.

"I don't want to hear that you are crying anymore, my dear," Usi's mother continued as she turned to Tiyan. "I am your mother now."

"Tiyan never lacked a mother, or father, or siblings. Chief Alile, our daughters, and I have been everything to her." Mrs Alile's voice held no malice.

Usi's mother ignored her. She sat down and urged Tiyan to sit on her lap. Tiyan hesitated and turned to look at Usi, who encouraged her to humour his mother's request. Gingerly, he placed Tiyan on his mother's lap, and she immediately embraced Tiyan, to the delight of Mrs Alile.

"This is wonderful!" she cried. "Tiyan, your future mother-in-law, has officially accepted you."

"Yes," Usi's mother declared. "I now have a daughter. I always wanted a daughter, and now I have one."

Usi helped Tiyan to her feet, and they moved to sit together on the sofa on the other side of the room as a maid brought them drinks.

"So, Chief Isekhure, when are you coming to see us officially?" Mrs Alile asked, and Tiyan cringed.

Usi was neither fazed nor annoyed. He smiled at her as he accepted a drink from the maid. "I don't think Chief Alile is ready for me, ma'am. But trust me, the minute he is, I will be there."

Mrs Alile's face revealed a hint of confusion. Tiyan stifled a groan. Her poor uncle would get an earful from his wife tonight. She smiled at the maid as she accepted a drink and took a sip.

"Mrs Alile, the delay is not from our end. My son is an honourable man. He has found his wife and is ready to do as tradition dictates, and he has my blessings. So go home and talk to Chief Alile."

Don't encourage her! Tiyan screamed inside. Oh, her poor uncle.

Thankfully, her aunt did not stay for dinner, not that Tiyan was surprised. She would need to go home, feed her husband, and give him an earful.

"Tiyan, are you planning a civil marriage ceremony after the Benin traditional marriage rites?" Usi's mother asked as they ate dinner.

Tiyan looked towards Usi, hoping for some assistance, but he ignored her and feigned deep interest in his meal. She turned towards his mother, smiling. "Usi and I have not decided. But I'm flexible, either way."

"Usi?" His mother glanced in his direction.

Serves him right!

Tiyan focused on her food as Usi raised his head from his

plate to look at his mother.

"Mum, we haven't got round to discuss the specifics. Knowing we are getting married is enough at present. Chief Alile hasn't even agreed to receive a bride price." He sounded a little irritated.

Tiyan raised her head and gave him a look that showed she was unhappy with how he had spoken to his mother. He obviously was in a bad mood because he returned her look with one that clearly said, *"Get over yourself; I don't care!"*

His mother did not press the matter; if she noticed the looks they exchanged, she said nothing.

"Tiyan, I thought we might spend some time together in the coming weeks going over the conventions surrounding being the wife of the chief priest."

Tiyan was glad about the subject change and smiled happily at Usi's mother. "Usi mentioned there were many rules and that you would teach me. That's very kind of you, ma'am. Thank you, I will look forward to it."

"I am glad to hear that. It would be my delight to teach you everything I have learnt. I will endeavour to make the experience painless, not the cumbersome experience my mother-in-law put me through."

Usi sighed and rolled his eyes while Tiyan, ignoring him,

smiled appreciatingly at his mother. "Thank you, ma'am."

"The pleasure is mine, my dear," Chief Mrs Isekhure said. "And it's mum now, not ma'am."

With that, she raised her glass and toasted with Tiyan, intentionally excluding Usi from the gesture.

"I am sorry if my mother was too much for you to handle. Bear with her. The idea of me getting married excites her greatly."

Usi offered an apology to Tiyan upon entering his house later that evening, after a time spent conversing with his mother about the forthcoming wedding, the date of which was still unknown to everyone.

Tiyan paused in the centre of the foyer, her eyes sparkling as she flashed him a warm smile. "You don't need to apologise. I like your mother. You sounded a little curt with her."

Usi grimaced and scratched his head. "She was asking questions I had no answers to. Questions she knows I have no answers to. I already explained to her that this is all new, and Chief Alile won't even hear of me taking steps towards the bride price payment."

Tiyan gently touched his arm. "Well, you said it yourself just now that she's excited. As she should be. You're her first son. If I can bear with her, so can you."

"Yes, ma'am." He put his arm around her waist, and they walked up the stairs together.

Tiyan glanced at him from the corner of her eye. "I think your mother is lovely, and I look forward to spending time with her as I learn the dos and don'ts." She wrinkled her nose.

Usi pulled her into his arms as they reached the first-floor landing. "If you feel overwhelmed, you will tell me, won't you?"

"Worried I might bail out on you?" Tiyan could not help but tease him.

"Anxious," he confessed, and the look on his face just melted her heart. "I must warn you again, being the chief priest's wife is not for every woman."

"I can imagine," Tiyan said, trying to lighten his mood. "Maybe I should run away now."

"This is my fear, so I want you to move in fully." He looked serious. "What do I have to do?"

Tiyan furrowed her brows as if deeply considering the matter. "Well, let's see. Maybe I'll move in if you promise to woo me and give me a marriage proposal like no other."

"You've got a deal," Usi affirmed, sealing the promise with a kiss.

As he drew back, his expression was grave. "My brother, Imagbe, arrives from the US tomorrow. He will be here until after the coronation ceremony. I will be away a lot as the coronation draws close. Expect little of my presence, as I'll be secluded, connecting with my ancestors and the gods. Then, I will be busy with the coronation ceremony and the traditional rites that must occur before, during and after. But I want you here the whole time.

"I will feel better knowing you are under my roof. My brother will ensure you have anything you need. It will be an excellent opportunity to learn about my family, as he's the revealer of family secrets. But if he becomes a nuisance, you have my permission to throw him out. He can go to my mother's."

Tiyan laughed outwardly, but within, her heart was racing. The experience of meeting his mother was not as bad as anticipated, but meeting his brother and becoming acquainted with said brother without Usi being around? Could she handle it?

It turned out that it wasn't only Usi's brother Ima Isekhure who arrived the following day from the US. Tiyan had gone home that morning to spend the day with Eki and Amenze. They were now counting down the days to Eki's traditional marriage ceremony and the coronation, and Eki needed much help. They dedicated the day to perusing fabrics and consulting with hairstylists and makeup artists. They visited the palace as Prince Osad had permitted Eki to remodel the queen's residence in the palace that was used by Osad's mother, Queen Esohe, and locked up since her death.

Eki toured the house with Tiyan and Amenze to help her decide what to keep and what to change. Aiai, an architect who designed the kitchen of every home she and her husband Efe Inneh built and sold, joined them, and they spent several hours inspecting the house and brainstorming what Eki could do with it. Money was no object. Osad had made that clear through his messengers.

It was an exhausting day, and when Usi's driver picked Tiyan up and took her to Usi's home, she hoped for a simple introduction to his brother, a quiet meal, and then bed. She was surprised that apart from Ima, two women about her age were present.

"And you must be Tiyan!" Ima smiled as he leapt from his chair and approached her. He resembled Usi but was slightly taller and had a lighter complexion.

Before Tiyan could say anything, she was hugged, lifted off the ground, and twirled. Almost as quickly, she was released, and Ima stood back to look at her.

"You're more beautiful than Usi claimed. I already told him to marry you quickly, or I'll beat him to it."

"*Uzuọ a*! Stop talking nonsense before I throw you out of my house!" Usi strode over to the pair.

As he did, he held out an arm to Tiyan, and as she moved closer, he encircled her waist, pulled her closer, and kissed her cheek. "How was your day?"

"Fine," she said, smiling up at him.

"This is my younger brother, Imagbe Isekhure. Ima, this is Tiyan."

Ima grinned at her. "Tiyan, I have heard many nice things about you from Usi and my mum. The woman is in love with you. You'll have to show me what spell you've cast on her so I can cast some of my own."

Usi rolled his eyes. "Try behaving."

With a chuckle, Tiyan extended a hand toward Ima. "Ima, it's a pleasure to meet you. Welcome home. I hope you had a pleasant trip, and I look forward to becoming better acquainted with you during your visit."

Before Ima had a chance to reply, the distinct sound of someone clearing their throat interrupted the silence. Tiyan, Usi, and Ima turned to see one woman had joined them. She was not very tall, even in her four-inch shoes, almost the same length as her fingernails, covered in green nail polish to match her green lipstick. She wore a simple, short, sleeveless pink dress, and as she turned to beckon on the other woman to join them, Tiyan realised it was backless with a bow at the small of her back.

"T, this is Esele Ebohon," Usi said. "Esele is the daughter of late Chief Ebohon, who was a priest and supported my father in his role as chief priest."

"Usi, Ima, and I have known each other since we were babies. We have known each other for so long that I cannot recall a time when Usi and Ima were not in my life." She placed an arm on each brother's shoulder and smiled at Tiyan, but her eyes were unfriendly.

The other woman joined them; Esele lowered her hands and briefly turned to acknowledge her companion before her gaze shifted to Tiyan.

"This is my friend, Nogie. Nogie Ehanire. She grew up with me and is well acquainted with Usi and Ima."

Tiyan smiled and extended her hand towards the two women. "Hello, Esele. Hello Nogie. It's lovely to meet you both."

"Hello, Tiyan." Nogie extended a hand towards Tiyan while Esele lifted her hands to adjust her stylish bob haircut, avoiding a handshake with Tiyan.

"Esele and I travelled together from the US," Ima said. "Nogie hasn't seen us in a while, so she raced here as soon as we arrived. And we invited her to join us for dinner."

"Oh, I see." Tiyan turned to Usi, who still had his arm

around her waist. "I thought your brother alone was expected."

"I accompanied Ima at the last minute. I wanted to catch up with Usi and see Nogie. Hence, I asked her to spend the night. Usi's home is our home. We come and go as we like." She shrugged.

"It's great to have you all here." Tiyan looked at Usi. "I should probably get changed for dinner, seeing as everyone is dressed up."

"We dressed up to go out for dinner, but since Usi can't be seen dining in public, we decided to stay home. He's promised us a fine dining experience and some dancing afterwards." Ima grinned.

Tiyan looked down at her jeans, denim shirt and Converse trainers. "I need to change. I'll be down in fifteen minutes."

"Take your time," Usi said. "Mrs Agbi is still setting up the dining room."

Tiyan stepped back from his embrace, offered a smile to everyone, and walked away.

CHAPTER NINE

As Tiyan quickly slipped into her black, form-fitting, off-shoulder dress and silver strappy stilettos, she pondered the nature of the guests, particularly Esele. The woman appeared unfriendly without any apparent cause. And she would stay here with Ima while Usi was away. Tiyan questioned her ability to cope. With Ima, yes. With Nogie, if she chose to stay on, possibly. With Esele? She doubted it, not after the brief encounter downstairs. If it all became too much for her, she could always go home, particularly if Usi was absent for half the time.

"I notice you're dressed in black, Tiyan," Esele commented during dinner. "Looks like you haven't yet learnt the dos and don'ts of being Usi's girlfriend."

"I don't think girlfriend is the word I would use in describing Tiyan. I have never thought of her as my girlfriend. And as for what she is wearing–"

"As for what she is wearing, cut her some slack, bro." Ima cut Usi off. "You take your chief priest role too seriously. Going out for dinner like regular people is not possible. Now, poor Tiyan can't wear what she wants. Tiyan, how will you survive being married to this chief priest?"

Tiyan smiled, turning to look at Usi, who was

visibly irritated. But before either she or Usi could respond, Esele cut in. "Since they are not married, she retains the option to decide that the life of a chief priest's wife is not suitable for her and choose to leave. If you can't handle the heat, leave the kitchen."

Tiyan gave Esele a sweet smile. "I am familiar with the saying, but leaving the kitchen isn't always the best choice. Certainly, the kitchen should have a window that can be opened to allow some air in and make the heat more tolerable."

Ima roared with laughter. "Bro, she is as intelligent as she is beautiful." He looked at Tiyan. "I am saying it again: if he doesn't marry you quickly, I will beat him to it."

"Get lost, fool!" Usi growled. He leaned closer to Tiyan, and she leaned in as they locked lips while the others watched in amazement.

"Usi, I never thought you would publicly show affection," Nogie remarked.

Usi's lips curved into a warm smile. "You don't know me as much as you think." He fed Tiyan a small piece of chicken.

Nogie's smile broadened as she observed him. Setting her wine glass aside, she began to clap enthusiastically. "I like this more relaxed version of you."

"Yes, me too," Ima responded, dabbing at the sides of his

mouth with his napkin. "It's preferable to the version of you that's uptight or the one who carries a chip on his shoulder for being the chief priest."

"Shut up!" Usi snapped.

"You ought to inform Tiyan that wearing black is not appropriate," stated Esele.

Tiyan's frown deepened as she gazed at Usi, yet the message in his eyes was clear—it was neither the time nor the place for questions, prompting her to keep silent.

Usi turned to Esele. "How my woman dresses and conducts herself is my business and no one else's."

His words weren't meant for Tiyan, but she decided to tread carefully around him for the rest of the meal. So did everyone else, and they ate quietly except Ima, who seized the chance to share with Usi about his life in America after Usi left.

After their meal, they descended to the basement, which housed the indoor pool and gym. Tiyan was surprised to see a DJ already set up by the poolside, blasting music through the loudspeakers. A table was arranged with various drinks and a selection of finger foods.

Tiyan gasped and turned towards Usi. "Ima wasn't kidding when he said you'd promised some dancing after dinner."

Usi shrugged. "Just because I can't socialise in public

doesn't mean I can't bring the party to my home."

"But isn't this a bit excessive for just five people?"

Usi shook his head. "Oh no. Ima and Esele have a few friends arriving soon."

Before Tiyan could respond, an exuberant Ima whisked her away to the poolside by the DJ, which seemed to be the unofficial dance area. Usi began to dance alongside Esele and Nogie. But when the music shifted to a slower, softer melody, Usi cut in and told Ima to get lost. He drew Tiyan into his embrace, and she yielded with ease.

Ima and Esele's friends arrived, and Ima rushed over to greet them enthusiastically, exchanging fist bumps and back slaps with the guys and warm hugs with the ladies. Usi and Tiyan ignored everyone else, completely absorbed in their own thoughts as they swayed to the music, locked in each other's embrace.

"I like your brother," she told him.

"He's a rascal. But he's a good kid. I like him too." He chuckled. "Besides, I am stuck with him. My mum always tells me I haven't got another brother."

"My mum used to tell me that whenever Osamu and I fought."

"You miss him a lot."

She pulled back to gaze into his eyes. "I do. Some days more than others."

"Even the fights?" he asked.

"Even the fights. Sometimes, I remember how he would throw away his leftover food whenever we fought instead of giving it to me. He disliked eating and was as thin as a stick. I enjoyed eating, and he always offered me his leftover food, but he threw it away whenever we quarrelled. In those moments, I would scream and cry for my parents, wishing they would come swiftly to save the food from ending up in the trash." She giggled.

Usi laughed. "Older brothers can be horrible. Or so I've been told." He touched her face. "I like how your eyes light up when you talk about them."

Tiyan nodded. Suddenly, her throat became tight. "For years, in my uncle's house, I was almost forbidden from talking about them."

Usi drew her closer, resting her head on his shoulder. "I can understand why they did that. But they were wrong. You can't heal that way. I want you to talk to me about them. I'll never get tired of listening."

Tiyan nodded without speaking, and Usi understood she was on the verge of tears.

"Let's get out of here." He grasped her hand and led her

out of the basement, ascending the stairs towards his bedroom.

Three days on, Tiyan remained in a deep slumber as Usi entered her bedroom through the concealed door within her dressing room, which linked her quarters to his suite.

She sensed his presence and opened her eyes to find him standing at the foot of her bed. With a smile and a stretch, she welcomed the new day. Usi approached and perched on the edge of the bed, leaning in to plant a gentle kiss on her forehead.

"Good morning. I am sorry I woke you up. I didn't mean to. I just thought I'd watch you sleep before leaving."

"That's creepy." Tiyan stifled a yawn, and Usi chuckled.

"It's not my fault you look so beautiful when you sleep."

Tiyan looked at his attire. He wore pristine white from head to toe, as he did most days when he dressed in traditional clothing. Yesterday, he informed her of his departure this morning for a five-day journey to seek guidance from ancestors and gods in preparation for the upcoming coronation ceremony.

"You're leaving now?" she asked.

He nodded. "Yes. Between Mrs Agbi and Ima, you'll be okay. I have left strict warnings that you are not to be upset while I'm away."

Tiyan eyed him playfully. "Have you now?"

"Yes, I have. And I left the warning in my chief priest voice, too."

"Oh. It terrifies me to imagine being on the receiving end of that voice."

"That voice is meant for everyone but you." Usi laughed softly, planted another kiss on her forehead, and then stood up straight. "I must leave now. I will see you when I return."

While Usi was away, Tiyan tried to keep to herself. She rose early and left the house before either Ima or Esele rose. Her days were spent with Eki and Amenze, and she returned to Usi's home late, so she missed having dinner with Ima and Esele. But she could not avoid them altogether as they didn't go to bed early. She typically accompanied them for post-dinner drinks, attempting to smile while they discussed their day and inquired about hers.

Ima was amiable, and despite his highly playful nature, unlike Usi's, Tiyan grew fonder of Ima each day. Esele was quite a different matter altogether. For reasons beyond Tiyan's understanding, the other woman disliked her and was highly critical of her actions. She was either displeased with Tiyan's attire, critical of how she spent her day, or she would speak at length about the duties of being a chief priest's wife.

"Do you think you can do this? Do you think you have what it takes to be the chief priest's wife?" she asked Tiyan at every opportunity.

The evening before Usi returned home, Tiyan came in late. Ima noticed her as she attempted to ascend the stairs quietly and called out.

"Hey, Tiyan, you're back! Come join us for a drink."

With a big smile, Tiyan entered the small reception room, which also served as a bar. Ima stood behind the bar, pulling a drink from the refrigerator.

"Been spending the day with your cousin again?" he asked, handing her a glass of sparkling ginger ale. Believing that she would adhere to her routine, he took her choice of drink as a given.

Tiyan smiled as she received the drink from him. "Thank you," she said and took a long sip. "Yes, I have been spending the day with my cousin Eki and our best friend, Amenze."

"You look exhausted. Sit down and put your feet up." He gestured to the leather armchair in the corner with its footrest. "I don't want Usi coming home tomorrow and giving me grief for not looking after you."

Tiyan chuckled, turning away from the bar, her drink in

hand. Esele was sitting on the couch next to the armchair, a glass of wine in one hand and her phone in the other. With her head lowered, she texted away and did not acknowledge Tiyan.

"Hello, Esele," Tiyan greeted as she lowered herself in the seat and propped her feet on the footstool. "Oh, wow! This is just what the doctor ordered."

"See. I told you that you looked tired," Ima said.

Esele raised her head and looked at Tiyan. "Hello, Tiyan. Have you been wearing yourself out again helping your cousin?"

"Yes," Tiyan responded. "We were at the palace working with interior decorators designing the interior of the queen's home."

"I hope they fed you?" Ima asked as he perched on a bar stool. "Otherwise, I might need to have a conversation with Osad."

Tiyan chuckled. Ima took his duty of looking after her in Usi's absence seriously. "Yes, they did. The palace kitchen catered to our needs. We had lunch and dinner before we left the palace."

Esele looked at Ima. "Tiyan is not a child," she said, turning to Tiyan. "It's nice of you to help your cousin prepare for married life. She's one lucky girl. She'll marry the king, enjoying glamour without your headaches."

"Esele, have you returned to discussing how challenging Tiyan's life will be after marrying Usi?" Ima sounded irritated. "What is your fascination with the idea of Tiyan marrying Usi? Leave her alone. As Usi mentioned recently, Tiyan's behaviour and attire are his concern and not the business of others."

At that, Esele shrugged and pouted. "I am just a concerned friend."

"Enough of the concern!" Ima snapped and turned his gaze towards Tiyan. "Listen, Tiyan, I won't lie; there are many protocols to follow. You will have more traditional protocols to follow than your cousin, who will be queen. However, since women before you have accomplished it, it surely isn't as complex as rocket science. If my mother can do it successfully, I'm confident you can, too."

"Thank you, Ima." Tiyan grinned and sipped her drink.

"Remember this: Usi is very intentional about everything he does. He would not have chosen you if he did not believe you possessed the qualities necessary to be his wife."

Esele snorted at that remark and turned her attention back to her phone. She did not join Ima and Tiyan's conversation, and both ignored her as they chatted.

Usi returned home early the following evening. Tiyan spent the day with Eki and Amenze, but she left early to be home when he arrived. She suspected he would return in time for dinner. She had missed him. Five whole days! She couldn't contact him as Usi turned off his phone while communing with the gods.

Tiyan showered quickly, dressed in snug black leather pants and a gold satin halter-neck blouse with a shimmer, and slipped on strappy gold sandals. She tied her hair into a ponytail and applied some makeup. Upon returning to her bedroom from the dressing room, she heard the sound of cars pulling up to the front of the house and slamming doors. Looking out the window, she spotted the guards who usually accompanied Usi. Excitedly, she raced out of her room and ran downstairs, ready to fling herself into his arms.

She halted outside the main doors, taken aback by Usi's stern look. Confused, she observed him withdraw and depart, likely aiming to take the private entry to his suite of rooms. The guards and drivers quickly dispersed, everyone avoiding her gaze.

What was wrong? Why had Usi behaved that way? Had he not missed her as much as she had missed him? Was he not happy to see her? Had something happened while he was away? Had he changed his mind about her? Did he not want her anymore?

"Is it your time?"

Tiyan turned at the sound of Esele's voice. Lost in her thoughts, she had not heard or seen the other woman approach and stand beside her. Wide-eyed, Tiyan gaped at her. It was her time. Her period had started three days ago.

She groaned. "Oh, no."

"Until it's over, you must avoid him."

"I completely forgot," she whispered. "But how did he realise?"

Esele folded her arms across her chest and scrutinised Tiyan from head to toe. "What kind of chief priest would he be if he couldn't sense it was your time? And especially when he's been in seclusion communing with the gods?"

Tiyan nodded. "He told me, but in my excitement, I completely forgot."

"And that brings me back to what I've been saying since I arrived. Are you cut out for this, Tiyan? This is one rule out of many, and you can't remember it. How will you remember the others? My father was a junior priest, but my mother struggled with the rules and the atonements for rule violations. It's a difficult life. I kid you not. Will you be happy?"

Tiyan hugged herself, her gaze fixed on the water fountain. Her eyes were fixed upon it, yet she neither saw nor appreciated its beauty as she once had. Her thoughts lingered on Esele's words, and Esele was far from finished.

"Can you live with being separated from your husband for

certain days every month when it's your time?" Esele continued. "Do you want a man who cannot take you out for a typical date night due to his role as the chief priest, which restricts his presence in certain public areas? Think about it, Tiyan. The demands associated with being the wife of a chief priest are considerable. And they will want to initiate you as an Olokun priestess, just like his mother. It will mean more rules and more restrictions on your life. I'm not cut out for that kind of life. I made that clear as an eighteen-year-old when Usi asked me to marry him."

Tiyan turned to gaze at Esele as though she had uttered complete nonsense. "Usi asked you to marry him?" This was news to Tiyan. She thought they had grown up together and were family friends. Was there more?

Esele wore a self-satisfied grin. "Yes, he did. His father chose me for him the moment I was born. It's the reason we grew up close together. It's why his father made provision for me to attend school in America like Usi and Ima. My father wasn't rich and could never have paid for me to be educated in the West. Usi's father made it possible. It was expected that we would marry, and when I turned eighteen, Usi presented me with a ring and vowed his eternal love for me. But I turned him down. At eighteen, I was smarter than you are. I told him I couldn't be a chief priest's wife. His father and mine asked him to give me some more time to grow up and get used to the idea of being a chief priest's wife."

Tiyan exhaled. "I see."

With nothing left to say, she spun around and returned to her bedroom. She was uncertain of her feelings. She experienced such intense embarrassment that her inclination was to burrow into a hole and remain there indefinitely. Had the guards and drivers been aware of the reason Usi had turned away from her? Had they known it was her time? Possibly. If Esele had guessed, then they very likely would have. The incident was the most embarrassing of the decade. How could she have failed to remember the rule about her period? She felt foolish.

This was going to be a lot harder than she thought. She liked Usi a great deal. But could she do this? Did she have what it took to be the wife of a chief priest? It was probably best she returned home and stopped seeing him. It was still early in their relationship; they could move on and find other people before their hearts became involved.

Concerning Esele, Tiyan also experienced a certain degree of embarrassment. Was she really pursuing a relationship with Usi right in front of the woman his family thought he would marry? Was Usi's mother among those who expected him to marry Esele? If so, why had she received Tiyan with open arms? What exactly was going on? First, Usi had not told her Esele was coming and then he had not told her the truth about their relationship, leaving her to assume the other woman was a family friend. A family friend his father desired as a daughter-in-law, so he financed her education abroad.

Tiyan groaned and sat on the bed. Was Ima in on this, too? Was he fostering her relationship with Usi, knowing that Usi anticipated Esele's acceptance of becoming his wife? What was going on? What was the truth? What was she doing with this man she knew so little about?

Usi had told her uncle he wanted to marry her and had been given permission to court her. But what about Esele? Or was he planning to marry them both? He could. He was a traditional chief priest, and if they only married according to Benin native law and customs, tradition permitted him as many wives as he could provide for.

But his father had not been a polygamist. Although that didn't matter, many men had no problems departing from what their fathers were. Usi may very well be considering polygamy. Unless he was using her to make Esele jealous and see what she was missing so she could make up her mind quickly. That made sense. And Esele, come to think of it, had been acting very much like the jealous lover from the moment she arrived, hadn't she?

Tiyan remembered his displeasure when his mother asked about a civil wedding ceremony. He had told her that his annoyance was that his mother asked a question he had no answer to. But could it be that his plan to marry her and Esele only according to Benin's native law and customs without a civil ceremony was the reason? A civil marriage ceremony would not allow polygamy.

But why would he bother with her at all? Why not just focus his energy on courting and marrying Esele? Or was all this to punish Esele for refusing him initially? Tiyan had no answers to all these questions. However, she understood that this relationship with Usi was advancing at an accelerated pace, and she lacked sufficient knowledge of him. It was time to take a step back. That step was to leave his home!

CHAPTER TEN

Hurriedly, Tiyan packed her bag. She didn't have many belongings with her, as she frequently brought clothes back to the house to swap them for different pieces from her wardrobe. Moments later, she wheeled her trolley case out of the house just as Ima arrived, pulling up in a white Lexus SUV owned by Usi. As he emerged, he appeared surprised to find Tiyan standing there with her large, wheeled suitcase.

"Tiyan, what's going on? Why are you leaving? I got a text from Usi's security detail saying he was home. Has there been a problem? Did you two fight?"

Tiyan was unprepared to revisit her conversation with Esele, Usi's outright rejection, or the embarrassment she experienced.

"Ima, I can't talk right now," she began, hoping he wouldn't push for information she wasn't ready to share. "I want to go home. Can you please call a driver, or will you take me?"

Ima was going to argue, but as he saw the tears welling up in her eyes, he changed his mind. "Okay. I'll take you anywhere you want to go, and then, if you're feeling like it, we can talk. If not, we'll talk tomorrow. Okay?"

Tiyan nodded as Ima guided her to the front seat of the

vehicle. A maid was already putting her bag in the back of the vehicle, and Ima got behind the steering wheel and started the engine.

As they approached the gate, there was no sign of it opening. The electronically controlled gate opened as cars approached unless the guard needed to question the driver and passengers. However, this typically occurred when a vehicle attempted to enter rather than exit. Additionally, this was one of Usi's vehicles, not an unfamiliar one.

As Ima brought the vehicle to a halt and waited for the guard to approach, Tiyan's phone beeped. She pulled it out of the tote bag and looked at it. It was a message from Usi.

Please don't leave me. I understand this is new to you, and you're feeling overwhelmed, but you will learn. I didn't mean to reject you openly. Forgive me. I promise to make it up to you.

Just as she finished reading the message, the guard approached the vehicle. Ima lowered the glass.

"I am sorry, sir," the guard began. "But Chief Isekhure has asked me not to open the gate. He wants you to return to the house with madam."

Ima swore under his breath and turned to look at Tiyan. "What do you want to do?"

"Ima, please. I want to go home. I need to go home to my

family now."

Ima swore under his breath again. "Open the gate, my good friend."

The guard looked towards the house and shook his head. "I am sorry, sir. But I can't disobey Chief Isekhure's instructions. Perhaps you should call him."

Ima took out his phone and called Usi, leading to a few minutes of intense argument between the two brothers. As the call ended, Ima turned to the guard and punched the steering furiously. "Open the gate!"

The guard glanced at the house, nodded, returned to his post, and pressed the button to open the gate.

Ima glanced briefly at Tiyan as he steered the vehicle out of the premises. "I am sorry. My brother can be as primitive as our father was. It's uncertain if it comes with the role of chief priest, but occasionally, he behaves as if he has never experienced life in the West."

Tiyan smiled at him. "Thank you. And I am sorry I caused you to fight with your brother."

Ima shrugged. "It's okay. We fight all the time. But we will settle. Mum will call us to her house for dinner, shed a tear or two and make us eat from the same plate, and all will be well again."

Tiyan couldn't help but burst out laughing, and Ima quickly joined in, their laughter filling the vehicle's interior.

When Tiyan returned home, thankfully, everyone was out, and she slipped in with her suitcase and proceeded to her room. She didn't need anyone asking her questions. Later that evening, after dinner, her uncle came up to her bedroom and informed her that Chief Isekhure was in the living room waiting to see her.

Tiyan's eyes widened. Usi was in her house? He wanted to see her? Had he forgotten it was her time?

"Is there a problem between you two?" her uncle asked.

"Er, no. There's no problem."

Chief Alile appeared unconvinced but chose not to pursue the matter further. "Go downstairs and attend to him. Close the door behind you to ensure your privacy. I will tell your aunt so no one disturbs you."

"Thank you, Uncle Zogie."

Tiyan refreshed her makeup and went downstairs to the living room, closing the door behind her upon entering. Usi stood to his feet. He looked handsome but tired in denim trousers and a polo shirt. Tiyan positioned herself at the furthest point from him that the confines of the room would permit.

She folded her arms across her chest. "Why are you here? You shouldn't be here. It's my time, and you said you can't be around me."

"Let me worry about that. It's my problem. I didn't mean to be curt earlier on. As I said in my text, this is a learning journey for you, but it is also a learning journey for me, and I will try to remember that you need my help and support. I didn't mean to embarrass you in front of others. I am sorry. Please come back to the house."

Tiyan shook her head. "Usi, I didn't leave because you embarrassed me."

"Oh." He frowned. "Did something happen while I was away? Did someone offend you? I did leave strict instructions that– "

"No one offended me. Not the way you think. I left because I'm unfamiliar with you, and things are progressing too quickly. I need to be on my own for a while to think about what I'm getting into."

"But you didn't think so before my trip. What changed?"

"I had a conversation with Esele. Suppose it can be called that. She was talking at me for the most part."

Usi's frown deepened. "What did she say?"

Tiyan looked at Usi. Esele had said a lot. From where did she begin? She threw her hands up in the air. "Why didn't you tell me she was more than a friend? That your father wanted you to marry her, and you proposed to her when she was eighteen? Didn't you think I should have been given such information?"

Usi's expression was one of complete astonishment. It took him a moment before he finally nodded in agreement. "If it were true, yes."

"You're saying that Esele is lying?"

"Yes!" Usi sounded angry. "If Ima or my mum were here, they would say the same thing. Esele has always been like a younger sister to me. My parents loved her as they had no daughter, and yes, when I was much younger, I was teased about being Esele's husband, but that's all that there was to it, and the teasing stopped as we grew older."

"But what about your father sending her to school in the US with you and Ima?"

"I was the first to go to school in the US. The moment I started secondary school, I was shipped off. Esele and Ima were three years behind me. When it was time for Ima to join me, Esele was inconsolable, so my father paid for her to come with Ima so we could all be together. As I said, my parents loved her like a daughter."

"You expect me to believe this?"

"Yes. I wouldn't lie to you," Usi said. "She's not the only girl child my parents have looked after over the years. You saw

Mrs Agbi's granddaughter, Ododo, in my mum's house the other day. My mum treats her like a daughter and intends to send her to America for her university education. Is that so I can marry her?"

He made some sense, Tiyan admitted as she chewed her bottom lip. However, Ododo's case was not the same as Esele's. Ododo was very young, and no one would expect Usi to wait for her. But Esele was a woman ripe for marriage. Tiyan sighed.

"I'm unfamiliar with you and your personality, so I left. For all I'm aware, you might have plans to wed us both.

Laughing bitterly, he shook his head. "Look at me, T. I am an exceedingly busy man. Between serving the gods, the king and the kingdom and managing my business, how much time do you think I have to be a husband to one woman, let alone two?"

"She said she declined your proposal due to concerns about being a chief priest's wife. She said your father and hers asked you to give her time to grow up and get used to the idea. Why would she lie?"

"How should I know?" Usi inquired, spreading his hands. "But I am damned if I don't find out before the night's over." He pulled out his phone, dialled a number, and spoke rapidly to someone.

Tiyan frowned as Usi ended the call and put his phone

away. "What's going on?" she asked.

"She will be here in a few minutes. Shall we sit down?"

Tiyan was rooted to the spot. "What do you mean she will be here in a few minutes?"

Usi sat down and patted the space beside him on the three-seater sofa. "Please come and sit, T. My guard and driver have gone to the house to fetch her. They will soon return."

"She's coming here?" Tiyan asked as she crossed the room and sat next to Usi.

"Is there any reason why she shouldn't come here?" Usi asked.

"No." Tiyan said. "It's just that–"

"Just that what?" Usi sounded like he was struggling to restrain his temper. "You said Esele told you I asked her to marry me."

"Yes. She did."

"Good. I want her here so she can say it again. This time while I am present to defend myself."

"Oh." Tiyan groaned, burying her head in her hands. This had turned out differently than she thought. She anticipated that he would deny everything and then depart, marking the conclusion of the matter. That's what most men would have done. But Usi Isekhure was not like most men.

Esele arrived in less than half an hour. She looked from Usi to Tiyan, and her eyes widened. Possibly because she recognised Usi was breaking traditional protocol by being near Tiyan while it was her time and perhaps because she suspected Tiyan had reported her to Usi.

"Tiyan, hi. Usi–"

"It is Chief Isekhure to you from now on, Esele." Usi's voice cut through the air like ice, so frigid that Tiyan hesitated to even glance in his direction. Esele froze to the spot, and the tension hung heavy in the room. "Please sit down and tell my wife again how I proposed to you when you were eighteen."

Esele didn't move. "I am sorry." Her voice was a whisper, and without looking at her, Tiyan could tell the other woman trembled.

"Esele, I will be annoyed with you in a minute. Tell my wife again how I proposed to you when you were eighteen."

"Tiyan, I am sorry. I–I–"

"You lied?" Tiyan asked.

Esele nodded. "I am sorry. I thought Usi would marry me. I thought–"

"I think we should go up to my room." Tiyan rose and extended her hand to Esele, who clutched it like a lifeline. Then,

Tiyan whirled to face Usi. "Please give us a moment."

In Tiyan's small upstairs bedroom, Esele broke down in tears and collapsed onto the bed. "I am sorry. I didn't mean to say the things I did. When I was young, I had a massive crush on Usi. My mother hoped we would marry and began preparing me to be Usi's wife. Then, when Usi's father decided to sponsor my education abroad, my mother and I took it for granted that it was a done deal. When he didn't make advances towards me, as I became a woman, I assumed it was because of his celibacy vow, but when I heard about you from Ima, I knew it was over.

"I came on this trip just to see you. I wanted to see the woman who took Usi from me. Please, don't take this the wrong way, as I don't mean this maliciously, but you're not beautiful. You're very light-skinned and men like that, but you're not as beautiful as I expected, and every day since my arrival, I have asked what he sees in you. What do you have that I don't have?"

Tiyan sat next to her and patted her knee. "I don't think that's how it works. Beauty is in the eye of the beholder. Someday, you will find that man who is right for you and thinks the sun rises and sets with you regardless of anyone else's thoughts."

Esele nodded as she pulled a pack of tissues from her purse and wiped her eyes. "I am done where he is concerned after what he's done tonight, breaking traditional protocol by sitting with you in your period and dragging me here. It's clear he loves you, and I won't bother you two anymore. I will go to my mother's until after the coronation. Hopefully, he doesn't stop my doctoral funding, and I can return to the US and get on with my life."

It was the first Tiyan heard that Esele was on a doctoral programme and that Usi supported her financially. He was likely continuing the work that his late father had started. In that case, it would not make sense to stop supporting her simply because she lied. She tried to assure Esele.

"I appreciate he's angry, but I don't think he's malicious enough to cut your funding. You are like his sister, after all."

Esele nodded and, for the first time, looked up and met Tiyan's eyes. "I am so sorry."

They both returned to the living room and as they entered, Usi stood, focusing solely on Tiyan.

"Are you coming with me?"

Tiyan shook her head. He looked sad, and she avoided meeting his gaze. "I need time. To think."

Usi nodded. "Take the time you need. I am at the main shrine all day tomorrow and return the day after. I will call you when I am back home."

As he turned to leave, Tiyan walked ahead to open the

front door, and Ima was on the other side, with a hand raised to ring the doorbell.

"Ima! Hello! What are you doing here?"

"Hello, Tiyan. Usi called me to pick up Esele." He looked past Usi and Tiyan to where Esele stood with her head bowed. "Come on, Esele, let's go."

As Esele walked past Usi and Tiyan, she turned to Tiyan with a small smile. "Good night."

Tiyan returned the smile. "Good night, Esele."

Usi looked at Ima. "Thank you for coming to get her."

"No problem, bro. Anytime," Ima said and turned to Tiyan. "My mum wants to see you tomorrow. She would be pleased if you could join her for brunch."

"I'd like that," Tiyan said. "Tell her I'll be there."

As Ima walked briskly towards the gate with Esele in tow, Tiyan and Usi followed at a much slower pace. They paused as they reached the gate and watched Esele and Ima enter the Lexus SUV and drive away.

"It will be wonderful to come home to you after leaving the shrine the day after tomorrow. I understand your need for time to think, and I won't pressure you. If you return to me, I want you to be certain you want this." He kissed her forehead. "I will send a driver to you tomorrow for your visit to my mother's and anywhere else you need to go."

Tiyan nodded, not sure she could trust herself to speak. Usi stepped out of the gate and into the Maybach while Tiyan closed the gate and returned to the house.

CHAPTER ELEVEN

"Tiyan! Come and hug me, darling child." Chief Mrs Isekhure smiled and stood up as Tiyan was escorted into the sitting room by a maid.

She looked stunning in a white cotton lace boubou gown and matching head tie, accessorised with white coral beads around her neck and wrists.

"Good morning, Mum." Tiyan curtseyed and moved closer to embrace the older woman.

Both women embraced warmly for a brief moment before stepping back.

"Please sit down," Usi's mother patted the seat next to her as she sat down. "Usi and Ima were here last night, yelling at each other, and then Usi left in anger, saying he was going to your house. Ima remained but didn't tell me much. He kept saying that Usi was acting like a primitive dictator and that the money spent on his Western education had been a waste. Then he got a call from Usi asking him to come to your house to pick up Esele before he killed her. My darling, what exactly is going on?"

Tiyan, with a smile, relayed the incident to Usi's mother, beginning with Usi embarrassing her openly and concluding with Esele's lie. When she was done, Chief Mrs Isekhure leaned back in her seat, her chin resting thoughtfully in her hand. A look of deep contemplation settled on her face as she gazed into the distance, lost in her own reflections. She cast a glance sideways at Tiyan, who was perched beside her, lost in thought.

"I want you to remember that I am not just Usi's mother. I was once married to a chief priest, and in the early days, I made many mistakes and broke many rules."

Tiyan arched an eyebrow, curiosity dancing in her eyes. "You did?"

Chief Mrs Isekhure laughed. "Of course I did. Did you think I was born the wife of a chief priest?"

Tiyan laughed, her eyes gleaming with anticipation. She was eager to hear every story that Usi's mother had to tell.

"I made countless mistakes," Chief Mrs Isekhure reiterated. "In the early years of my marriage, even after the birth of my two sons, I constantly found myself making mistakes. And it didn't help that I had a mother-in-law from hell. She was as impatient as she was critical. You didn't quit your marriage in my day, so I stayed, learnt, and improved. Now, the rules have become second nature; I adhere to them instinctively."

Tiyan nodded. It was clear that practice could lead to perfection and that, with time, anyone could master what they regularly practised.

Chief Mrs Isekhure leaned closer and took Tiyan's hands in hers. "What happened yesterday was a mistake. You were excited. You missed him and wanted to welcome him home. But unfortunately, Usi is not like most men. Protocols exist for something as simple as going out to greet your man when he returns home."

Tiyan lowered her gaze as she recalled the moment Usi turned from her and the embarrassment she endured from being rebuffed in the presence of the drivers and guards.

"I completely forgot it was my time. Well, I didn't forget it was my time. I just forgot what it meant where Usi is concerned. Is it a rule that applies to all women? Women can't be around him when it's their time?"

Chief Mrs Isekhure laughed as she released Tiyan's hands. "No. Of course not. That would be absurd. It applies solely to you as his wife. Other women don't have the same effect over him, so it wouldn't matter if they were in their period and around him."

"But I am not yet his wife," Tiyan protested.

"I recognise your bride price has yet to be paid, but Usi has claimed you as his, and as chief priest, it means the gods have put their stamp of approval on the union even though the bride price hasn't been paid."

Tiyan sighed. "This is not going to be an easy journey. Esele talked about all the rules, and later, when she and I talked, I learnt her mother had been training her. It left me feeling inadequate like maybe he should be with her instead."

"Whether he should or shouldn't be is no longer relevant. Usi has chosen you. Whatever Esele has learnt about being the chief priest's wife, I hope she finds it beneficial in other aspects of her life. You are the chief priest's wife and will acquire the necessary knowledge. Usi also needs to learn. As he correctly pointed out, he needs to learn to be supportive while you acquire the essential knowledge. As for Esele, please extend your forgiveness to her. She wanted Usi, but he prefers you, and the heart understands its own desires.

"She might have had an opportunity with Ima, but the lies she told, coupled with her admission of having feelings for Usi, mean that Ima will not consider her now. But she must not be Mrs Isekhure. There are other wonderful Benin families from which she can marry. Let's put that ugly incident in the past where it belongs. Please don't let it ruin your relationship with Usi. I want you to think about what he did yesterday. If he broke a sacred traditional protocol to come and see you and set things right with you, I think he deserves for you to commit to making this relationship work, and that's all I ask."

Tiyan nodded to show understanding, and Usi's mother

squeezed her hand gently. "He's preparing for the coronation, Tiyan. If you leave him, he will be devastated. It might disrupt his focus, leading to an error. Remember that he is first a man before a priest. As a man, he is vulnerable because he cares for you."

A maid entered the room and announced that brunch was ready and set up on the front balcony. Ima barged in as Chief Mrs Isekhure and Tiyan stood up to step outside.

"Hi, Mum!" he greeted excitedly, lifting his mother and twirling her around just as he had done with Tiyan on the day they first met.

Chief Mrs Isekhure erupted into laughter, a sound so infectious it felt like the joy of a child. She playfully smacked her younger son's arm, her eyes sparkling with delight.

"Such a silly boy!" she exclaimed as she glanced at Tiyan. "If you had been involved with this son of mine, we wouldn't be having this conversation. I would have advised you to seek a different man."

The trio burst into peals of laughter.

After brunch, Ima accompanied Tiyan to her car, providing an opportunity for a brief chat.

"I want to apologise for what Esele did. Usi told me that's why you left. I had no idea. I would have set you straight if you had only told me that day. I feel terrible because I should not have let Esele accompany me on this trip."

"It's not your fault, Ima. How could you have known her motives when she requested to join you?"

Ima gave a casual shrug with his hands tucked into the back pockets of his jeans. "In hindsight, I see how I could have known. Her interest piqued the moment I mentioned that Usi had found his wife. She asked numerous questions I couldn't answer, as I'd never met you. Then she said she would meet you when we visited Benin. This was the first time she expressed interest in accompanying me on the trip, and I surmised she wanted to meet you because she regards Usi as an older brother figure." He sighed and shook his head. "She won't be bothering you again. I drove her to her mother's last night."

Tiyan offered a brief smile to the driver as he held the door open for her before she redirected her focus to Ima. "Yes. She did say she would go there."

"So, are you coming back soon?" he asked.

Tiyan reached out and affectionately squeezed his arm. "Soon," she assured him, climbing into the back seat of the Maybach. The driver shut the door.

Tiyan nestled in her bed that night, her mind swirling with

thoughts of her relationship with Usi. Memories of laughter and tender moments filled her head, but the questions lingered, urging her to ponder what the future held for them. Usi's actions the other night cleared doubts about his relationship with Esele. And if any doubts remained, her chat with his mother and Ima had removed them. But was that enough? Was Usi the right man for her?

She had lost her immediate family, and if she was going to get any semblance of happiness in the future, she had to pick a man with whom she could create a family that would be just as happy, if not happier, than the family she'd lost. Neither polygamy nor a loveless marriage appealed to her. She required assurance that her marriage would be free of both before she could accept a marriage proposal.

Usi appeared confident that she was the right one for him. However, was she certain that he was the right one for her? If he wasn't, then who was? Thus far, she had not met anyone who could compare.

Tiyan sighed, restless in her single bed. Maybe she was overthinking things. What was the problem? Yes, family was important to her, and she sought the right man to create that family with, but who was to say that man wasn't Usi? Thus far, he had given her no reason to doubt they could build a happy family together.

Usi had stepped in to resolve the issue with Eki. He had visited her, despite it being inadvisable, to resolve their conflict. He dragged Esele to her house to demonstrate he was telling the truth. His mother and brother corroborated his story. What more did she want?

If she had a limited understanding of him, wasn't that the reason for this courtship? She would go back and allow herself to be wooed and courted. She would not rush into marriage but would not stay away either. His mother believed he cared deeply for her, and no one else could comprehend her son like she did. Also, Esele admitted that Usi was in love with her. That could not have been easy for the other woman to say, and she wouldn't have said it unless it was true.

Tiyan smiled and shut her eyes. She would go back tomorrow, she decided as she gave in to sleep.

The following day, she arrived at Usi's home just after lunch. She wanted to make him dinner before he came home. Her period was now over, so she could do that. She yearned to see his reaction. Mrs Agbi was a little reluctant to relinquish her kitchen and duties, but Tiyan assured her this was just a one-off and she wouldn't make it a habit to take over the other woman's kitchen or duties.

The kitchen was a big white affair. The entire space gleamed in pristine white, from the sleek marble floor and countertops to the cutting-edge kitchen appliances and the sturdy oak counter stools. It was a part of the house Usi had not shown her the day he had taken her around the house, perhaps because he didn't want to step on Mrs Agbi's toes. Tiyan shook with laughter as she walked towards the double-door American-style refrigerator. She took a quick peek inside and decided on what she would make for dinner.

Usi switched on his phone, intending to text Tiyan, but changed his mind. It was probably too soon. She had asked for time to think, and he promised she could take the time needed. Besides, he was just coming out of the shrine where he had been the last twenty-four hours plus, inducting new priests and leading old and new priests in prayers for the incoming king. He needed to get home, rest, and break his fast before anything else.

If he was sure that she was his, and he was, then he had to give her the time and space she needed to reach the same realisation herself. He had to be careful not to appear to pressure her in any way. He called his brother instead.

"Ima, *woyeh*? How are you?" he asked as Ima's voice came on the other end of the phone.

"Hey, Usi. I'm good, bro. Are you home?"

"Not yet. On my way. I just left the shrine," Usi

responded. "Have you been in touch with Tiyan?"

"Yesterday, she was at Mum's for brunch as promised."

Usi nodded. "And?"

"And she left. She promised she'd come to the house soon." There was a pause. "Do you need me to come over now? I am hanging out with my friends. But I can come home and join you for dinner and a board game."

"No. You hang out with your friends. I'm good," Usi said. "I'm exhausted anyway, so I'll have an early night."

He disconnected the call and berated himself. *What were you hoping to hear, idiot?* He asked.

From the moment Usi climbed out of the car and into the house, he was irritable. The servants quietly moved out of his way as he entered the foyer and ran up the stairs to his private suite of rooms. An hour later, he went downstairs to the dining room, freshly showered and dressed in grey jogger bottoms and a white T-shirt.

He pushed the door open, entered the room, and froze. Tiyan was wearing an apron over a denim shirt dress and setting the table. He was uncertain about how to respond to that. Why was she in Mrs Agbi's apron? Why was she setting the table? Where was Mrs Agbi? Where were the maids?

Tiyan glanced up from arranging the table and offered a

smile to Usi, who seemed rooted to the spot in fascination.

"Hi. Welcome back. How was your day?"

"You sound like the little lady of the house." He extended his arms, drawing her close, as their lips met in a prolonged kiss. "You're back?"

Tiyan nodded, and he kissed her once more. When he pulled back, he looked at the table.

"What's going on?"

"I made dinner."

He furrowed his brows. "Why? Where is Mrs Agbi?"

"I let her have the evening off. I wanted to make you dinner. You don't mind, do you?"

"Goodness, no. I am thrilled that you cooked. I just don't want you slaving over a hot stove. That's not why you're here."

Tiyan nodded. "Mrs. Agbi expressed the same sentiment. It took a lot to convince her to let me have her duties and kitchen for the evening. Speaking of which, she better not see me wearing her apron."

Usi laughed, and Tiyan joined in the laughter. "So what did you make?" He eyed the table. "Looks like you've put yourself through much trouble."

"No trouble at all," Tiyan assured him, gazing at the table

covered with dishes of varying sizes. "There's some pepper soup for the starter course, and I baked some bread rolls. They're fresh and hot from the oven."

"Hmmm… baker's daughter. I would love to try that."

"Good. That's what I like to hear." Tiyan took off her apron. "I'll be back in a moment." She left the room and returned the apron to the kitchen. When she came back, Usi was holding out a chair for her. She sat down, and he pulled out a chair and sat beside her.

"So, what else have you got here?"

"There's some coconut rice with some dodo and gizzard and chicken stew to go with it. Alternatively, there's plantain fufu and black soup. And I have a platter of spicy snails. For dessert, I made a sponge cake and some custard."

"Let's eat. I'm tasting it all."

"I love it when you're a good sport." Tiyan leaned closer to him.

Usi leaned closer so their lips were only an inch apart. "I am always a good sport where you're concerned," he murmured and touched his lips to hers.

As they ate, Tiyan asked about Esele. "You are not going to stop her funding, are you?"

Usi shook his head as he opened the bottle of sparkling

grapefruit juice. "As long as she keeps to her end of the bargain, to stay away from my home and you, I see no reason for such a drastic measure."

Tiyan sipped her drink, wrinkling her nose as the bubbles tickled her nostrils. "Your anger is scary. I wasn't on the receiving end, but I was scared."

Usi filled up his glass and turned to her. "You have no reason to be scared. I can manage myself and my anger, T."

"Oh," Tiyan said, not sure what else to say. She busied herself, serving Usi some pepper soup.

"This is delicious," he said after he had tried some soup and bread. "You're the complete deal: beautiful, intelligent and a great cook. What more could a man ask for?"

Tiyan laughed. "I won't take that compliment lightly after your taste buds have become accustomed to eating Mrs Agbi's food." Her phone beeped on the table beside her, and she glanced at it. It was Mr Orobator calling. She sighed as she rejected the call and switched off the phone. "Sorry about that."

Usi frowned as he buttered some bread. "Is there a problem?" As Tiyan drank her soup and delayed answering, his frown deepened. "T?"

Tiyan put down her spoon and sipped from her glass of water. "It's Mr Orobator, Ekpen Orobator, who rents my parent's home and my mother's bakery."

"What does he want?"

"He wants to buy both properties: the house and the bakery," Tiyan said. "He's been bugging me forever."

"And you don't want to sell?"

"No, I don't." *How could she*? "My mother wanted me to join her in the business. I told you this the first night I was here. She's dead, but I would still like to regain control of the bakery someday and run it and expand it, knocking down the wall between the bakery and the house. But when my parents passed away, nobody was aware of my plans, and Uncle Zogie leased the house and the bakery to this man, Mr Orobator, who my mother employed. He gave it away for a pittance to get the money to care for me. The man was interested in buying, and Uncle Zogie promised he would be able to as I am a girl and would marry and not need the properties. Uncle Zogie was desperate to find one person who wanted both the house and the bakery."

Usi nodded to show understanding. "When you were old enough to decide, you said you weren't selling?"

"Yes. And he kept hounding me. At one point, when Eki and Amenze were going to go to the UK for their MBA, I wanted to sell the house and bakery so I could afford to go with them, but then Eki decided that since Eseosa didn't want to go to the

UK for a master's, she would sponsor me. She had much money at her disposal due to Oba Edoni's generosity. So I called Mr Orobator and told him I wouldn't sell. Since my return, he's constantly contacted me by phone and text, claiming that my uncle and I reneged on our promise.

"It's stressing me out. He's hinted that he wants to marry me, and I think he just wants to take possession of the properties. The last few days, he's insisted I come to the bakery to talk and resolve the matter, or he will go to the native court. He claims the native court will rule in his favour as I am a woman. I have asked to meet elsewhere, but he has refused, and the last time I saw him at the bakery when no one else was there, he, he–"

Usi frowned. "He what?"

"He touched me inappropriately and forced me to kiss him."

Usi's hands stilled while serving some snails on his plate. "When did this happen?"

Tiyan shuddered slightly as her mind returned to that awful moment when she had gone to see Mr Orobator to collect the rent, which she needed to purchase a few things for school as a fresh undergraduate.

She sipped her glass of sparkling grapefruit juice, wishing it was alcohol. "A few years ago."

Usi nodded. His attention was on his plate, but Tiyan could tell from the slight shaking of his hand as he picked up his cutlery that he was trying to control his anger. "How old were you?"

"Seventeen." Tiyan sighed as she put down her glass. "It put me off men altogether. Until you, I never wanted a man to touch me."

"You didn't tell your uncle?"

"No. I didn't want to cause any trouble."

"I see. Well, you leave it with me. I think I am better equipped than you are to deal with such men." Usi looked at her. "Don't answer his calls, don't respond to his texts. Don't meet him anywhere. Do not engage with him at all."

Tiyan nodded and didn't argue.

"The coronation ceremony is at hand, but once it is over, I will sort this fellow out," he promised.

CHAPTER TWELVE

Usi looked around him as his driver drove into a gated neighbourhood and parked in front of a grey bungalow with grey gates. This was where Tiyan grew up. It was a neighbourhood that was unfamiliar to him. He could not remember ever coming to this part of the city.

It was a far cry from the neighbourhood where he was raised, and where he now lived in a corner among the rich, his house elevated, so he looked down at the city from his bedroom balcony. What a great price he had paid for that privilege.

"We have arrived, Chief," the driver informed him, and he grunted in response. He looked around him again. By and large, it was a decent neighbourhood. He pushed his Ray-Ban sunglasses down the bridge of his nose and peered closely at the house before moving his gaze to the building beside it. The gate was non-existent, possibly because it was used for commercial purposes. A floor-to-ceiling glass covered the front, and a bold inscription read Alile's Bakery.

Tiyan had told him that, as part of the deal made with her uncle, Mr Orobator was not allowed to change the bakery's name until he had bought it. Several cars were parked in front of the building, and customers entered and exited through a glass swing door.

It had been three weeks since Tiyan had told him about Mr Orobator. As they approached the coronation, he was with her on more than one occasion when Mr Orobator called or texted. Usi had barely been able to contain himself. With the coronation over, it was time to deal with this Orobator fellow once and for all. In the last few weeks, he had pondered the matter.

As chief priest, he dealt with many land disputes. In the native court, he presided as judge. He could tell the man to get lost as he had no claim to a land that rightfully belonged to Tiyan and any children she would bear, but he had to tread carefully. As much as he opposed Orobator buying Tiyan's inheritance, he had to ensure that for his name and position, he dealt as fairly as possible, or people might accuse him of throwing his weight around and being oppressive. And that would not be a good thing. As chief priest, he had a duty to serve the people and not to use his office and the power that came with it to oppress them.

His driver opened the door, and he climbed out of the car, muttering his thanks and smoothing his wrapper. He had chosen to come dressed in traditional attire, so he wore his white wrapper, the traditional white short-sleeved shirt on which the *Ada and Eben* royal sceptres were embroidered, and white Italian designer shoes.

As he approached the bakery, a man rushed out. He was slightly shorter than Usi, with a beer belly, and wore grey pants and a navy shirt. Usi instantly knew he was the Mr Orobator and guessed he was about forty. He appeared excited to see the chief priest in his business premises and was smiling and bowing slightly as he approached. Usi disliked him on sight.

So, this was the man harassing his woman to sell her inheritance? This man had brokered a deal with Chief Alile, who had no head for business and had ripped Tiyan off all these years. He was giving her a measly rent when she should have been getting a profit from the business.

This was the man who sexually molested her and then turned around years later to hint at marrying her. Usi knew he did it to gain control of the properties. He was a terrible man who had taken advantage of the pain and suffering of others. Usi wished he was not in a position of authority so he could deal with him like the rogue he was.

"Chief Isekhure, good afternoon. What brings you to my office?"

Usi removed his pair of Ray-Bans and narrowed his eyes, ignoring the hand the man had stretched out. Did he not know tradition?

"I am here on behalf of my woman," Usi said. "Let's talk in your office."

"Of course, Chief." Mr Orobator led the way into the building.

As they entered the bakery's front-of-house, the enticing scent of freshly baked goods enveloped Usi's senses, almost tempting him to stop and indulge. Some customers sat at tables, sampling the baked goods, while others waited to be served. The service area was buzzing with activity as three uniformed staff members hustled to attend to the needs of the customers. There was a door at the end of the public area with the inscription, Staff Only. Mr Orobator opened the door and ushered Usi into a much smaller room with a cluttered desk and several chairs.

"Please, sit down, Chief Isekhure," Mr Orobator waved to a chair on the other side of the desk as he sat behind the desk and rubbed his hands together, grinning like the Cheshire cat. "It's an honour to have you in my office. So how can I help you, Chief?"

Usi reclined in his chair, biting the arm of his sunglasses as he studied the man before him. "As I said outside, I am here on behalf of my woman."

Mr Orobator appeared puzzled. "Your woman?"

"Yes. Tiyan Alile."

Mr Orobator swallowed and shifted uneasily in his chair. "Oh. I had no idea she was your woman, Chief Isekhure."

Usi nodded. "I understand that you were unaware, which is why I am not annoyed that you are texting her constantly. While we are eating and even in bed."

Mr Orobator brought out a handkerchief and wiped his brow. "I am very sorry, Chief Isekhure. It will not happen again."

"You are right. It won't. I am here to sort the matter and ensure you stop bothering her. When you bother her, you bother me," Usi said. "As I mentioned earlier, I am not annoyed yet. But I will be if, after today, you continue to disturb her. I am here so we can talk, one man to another. What is it you want? My woman does not wish to sell the properties, the house and the bakery."

Mr Orobator nodded. "Yes, she mentioned this. But you see, about eleven years ago, when I was going to rent both properties, Chief Alile assured me that the properties would be sold to me when Tiyan was old enough to do so. Otherwise, I would not have rented them."

Usi clasped his hands on his lap. "Mr Orobator, I do not like that you address my wife by her first name."

"I am sorry, Chief Isekhure. I meant to say, Miss Alile."

"I am sure that's what you meant to say. And that brings me to the next issue. At the time of the original transaction, did you make Chief Alile an offer to buy the properties?"

Mr Orobator laughed awkwardly. "Absolutely not! I could

not possibly have done that. I didn't have the funds."

"But now you have the funds?" Usi asked.

"Yes." Once again, Mr Orobator grinned like the Cheshire cat. "Business has been good over the years."

"And was your rent increased?"

"No. But I have paid it without fail through the years."

Usi nodded. "I see. So, you were given the properties to rent at the time, and although you would have liked to buy them, you couldn't afford them. But now that you can, you harass my wife to sell to you?" Before he could answer, Usi continued. "And I don't want to mention the incident in this office the last time she was here. Let's not talk about it, shall we? Or I will become very annoyed."

Mr Orobator became very quiet. "Yes, Chief Isekhure."

"Good," Usi said. "Here's what we are going to do. I have a house, a duplex, the same size as these two houses, in a choice area in town. I will give it to you at the asking price for these twin bungalows. You can live there and establish a bakery there or any other business. But you have three weeks to pay for it and vacate these premises."

"But Chief Isekhure, three weeks is a very short time."

"Three weeks, my good friend, or you lose the offer, which, if you ask me, is very generous indeed." Usi rose and placed a card on the table. "That's my business card; call me if interested."

"Yes, sir." Mr Orobator collected the card and followed Usi behind as he walked out of the building towards his Mercedes Maybach. The driver was standing with the back door open.

As Usi reached the car, he turned to face Mr Orobator and removed his Ray-Bans so the other man could see his eyes.

"My wife has been stressed lately and is resting. I don't want you calling her to bother her or ask her to reason with me. I don't want you calling my woman or texting her again. Please don't call, don't text, don't talk to her, don't put your hand on her and don't even lust after her. Do you understand me? She is mine and off-limits. Mess around with my woman again, and I will turn you into a goat."

He didn't spare Mr Orobator another glance as he put on his sunglasses and got into the car. The driver closed the door before taking the wheel.

A few days later, Usi received a call from Mr Orobator requesting to view the property on offer. The same day, he made full payment for the property. Usi was not surprised. A man like that knew a good deal when he saw one. Usi did not speak to Tiyan as he wanted to get the keys to both properties first.

She had no idea what he had been up to. He told her that

he was dealing with the Orobator problem and said no more. To show she trusted him, she had not once asked what he was doing, how he intended to handle it, or when there would be a result.

He assigned a personal staff member to follow up with Mr Orobator as he moved his family out of Tiyan's childhood home and quit the bakery. Usi made sure that Mr Orobator could only depart with the baking equipment he had bought over time. All the equipment that was present when he assumed control of the bakery was still there.

Tiyan wouldn't need them, as Usi intended to ensure she had the money to buy her own equipment, the latest and best in the market. Still, they were hers, and Usi had no intention of letting Mr Orobator take them with him. He also ensured that Mr. Orobator paid a rental fee for the equipment and a depreciation charge.

Mr Orobator seemed eager to get rid of Usi because he did everything he was required to do quickly. Within three weeks, Usi received the keys to the properties. The bakery was still up and running, as he had given the staff who wished to remain an incentive until Tiyan decided what she wanted to do. So, to customers, nothing had changed; Alile's Bakery was still operational.

He was glad when he could finally go home to Tiyan and hand her the keys to the properties and a cheque for the amount

Mr Orobator had paid for the new property.

As they cuddled together on the wicker corner sofa on the balcony outside his bedroom, he passed her an envelope with the cheque and the keys to the bakery and house. He watched as she sat up straight and opened the envelope, looking at the keys and the cheque in amazement.

"What is this, Usi?" she asked. "What's going on?"

"The keys to the house and the bakery. Mr Orobator has moved out. The bakery and house are yours again to do as you like."

Tiyan was thrilled. She flew into Usi's arms and kissed him repeatedly. "You are my superstar," she said in between kisses. "How did you do it? You didn't go there throwing your weight around as a settler of land disputes, did you?"

Usi chuckled. "Of course, I didn't. Why would I? I made him an offer he couldn't refuse. The new property is in the highbrow area, which is better for his family and any business he decides to start. He can start a bakery. Whatever he wants to do. And I offered it to him at the asking price for your property. It was a very good deal. I also negotiated for the staff to remain and your mother's equipment and ensured he paid a hire fee and depreciation fee."

"Wow!" Tiyan said. "You didn't go easy on him at all."

Usi sat up. "I was a lot easier on him than I wanted to be, T. The man is a rogue who exploited you and your uncle. He took a fully functional bakery with staff, equipment, customers, name and goodwill and did not pay a dime. He paid rent. What's that? He should have been giving you a share of the profit yearly, at the very least. But what's done is done. You have the place back. The staff and the equipment."

Tiyan kissed him again. "Thank you so much, Usi." She looked at the cheque and then at Usi. "What's this for?"

Usi shrugged. "I want you to have the money he paid for the new property."

"But I can't," Tiyan protested. "That's your property, and this is a lot of money."

Usi exhaled deeply. He had known she would be difficult. "It was my property. But not anymore. I planned for you to have it and swap it with your father's property. And keep the money from the sale. So now you get to keep your father's house, and you get to keep the money from the sale of the other house."

"But, Usi–"

"Don't argue with me, T. I know what I am doing. You're a first daughter and now the only surviving child of your father. His name, his legacy, and his entire bloodline rest on you. You are responsible for ensuring his place in this kingdom and his community. And the day I claimed you as mine, by tradition, that responsibility became mine. You have great dreams for the bakery and the house, but you need money, and the money from the house sale will help you bring that dream to fruition. So, I do not want to hear another argument."

"Okay, Usi," Tiyan let out a sigh and offered him a smile. "Thank you, but no more gifts."

Usi laughed yet made no promises, and Tiyan rolled her eyes and shook her head. There would be more gifts. She knew it. But this gift she would treasure. This gift allowed her to fulfil the dream that had been her mother's and was now hers.

Now that Mr Orobator was out, Tiyan planned to renovate the bakery and extend it to the house. She would view the place tomorrow and set her plans in motion.

CHAPTER THIRTEEN

Six months later…

"Happy birthday, T."

Tiyan opened one eye and then the other. She looked at Usi, standing at the edge of her bed dressed in his white pyjamas and dressing gown. She stretched languidly, grinning from ear to ear. "Thank you. You remembered."

Usi snorted. "Remembered? Are you kidding me? I have thought of nothing much else for the last few weeks."

Tiyan shook with laughter as she started to sit up in bed. He was right. The planning for her twenty-fifth birthday party had been going on for the last six weeks or more. Usi wasn't playing about this party. He knew she had not had a party since she was thirteen, after which her parents and brother were killed.

She had not wished to celebrate or trouble her uncle with something as frivolous as a birthday party. Usi said this was a make-up for all the parties she'd not had for over a decade. He was fully set to throw her a big party. Last night, before she retired to bed, the decorators had been around to start turning the large foyer downstairs into the perfect party venue.

The finest caterers in the city were hired, and Mrs Agbi

had been working with them for the past month to select the menu and ensure everything was perfect for the high-profile guests expected, including the Oba and his Oloi, Eki. The guests had been informed to get ready for an unforgettable experience with an amazing DJ, a live band, and a celebrity MC all set to make the event truly spectacular! This left no doubt in anyone's mind that she was his chosen one.

"I have something to show you."

Tiyan frowned. "Now?" she asked, climbing out of bed.

"Yes, now." He sounded impatient.

"Okay, give me a moment to freshen up." Tiyan slipped on her pink dressing gown over her nightgown and raced into the bathroom.

A few minutes later, she was standing with Usi on the balcony outside his bedroom and watching, with tears in her eyes, as a Benin cultural group of singers, dancers, and drummers performed a happy birthday song for her. They were a sight to behold: the women in red wrappers tied across their chests, their hair styled in the traditional *okuku* hairstyle and dripping in coral beads, and the men, shirtless in white wrappers tied around their waists, with coral beads on their necks and wrists.

In their hands, the women held the *ukuse*, a traditional Benin musical instrument made of small beads strung together around a gourd. They sang her praises in the Benin language even as they wished her many happy years ahead and fulfilment as a wife and mother. As they finished their brilliant performance, Tiyan waved her thanks and prepared to leave, but Usi tightened his grip on her.

"I have something else for you," he whispered.

Tiyan turned her head toward the cultural group, who were starting to disperse from the driveway. Behind them, a vehicle approached slowly, driving up from the car park towards the front of the house. It was a white Range Rover Evoque, and Tiyan gasped as she saw the letters "TIYAN" on the customised number plate.

"Happy birthday, my love," Usi whispered, and Tiyan began to cry.

"Usi, it's a car!" she said. "That's a car!"

Usi chuckled. "I should certainly hope so because I ordered a car."

Tiyan laughed through her tears and dropped her head on his shoulder. "Usi, you are like a dream. You're too good to be true."

Usi lifted her head and, with his thumbs, gently brushed away her tears. "I am just a man who is helplessly and hopelessly in love with you. I thought I was the first night I came to you, but with every passing day, I have had a chance to know you better, I have come to the startling realisation that my heart is yours forever." He bent his head and kissed her.

And there it was, finally. The words she had yearned to hear for months. If Tiyan had doubted Usi's love, any doubt had been removed the last six months as they had settled into their relationship following the resolution of Esele's lies and the problem with Mr Orobator and Tiyan's parents' properties.

First, he had not rushed her or pressured her into marriage. She had thought that after helping her secure her childhood home and her mother's bakery and giving her the money from the sale of his house, he would confess his love and propose to her, but he had not.

He took her on a little trip to the places she had mentioned in passing that she would like to visit. She was touched by the fact that he paid close attention to everything she said. They were gone for ten days, and with one of the royal jets at his disposal, Usi took her to the Maldives, Amalfi Coast in Italy, and Santorini, Mykonos and Corfu in Greece.

They spent their days sightseeing and swimming and their nights dining and dancing away in nightclubs. It had been a memorable experience. She had seen a different side of Usi, a more relaxed side, that he didn't show in Benin.

When they returned from that trip, he supported her as

she worked to renovate and extend the bakery, buy new equipment, and hire more staff. His actions were those of a man in love. Others saw it and pointed it out, but Usi said nothing. And that began to bother Tiyan. She had wanted to be courted and wooed, and so far, Usi had done that.

She had been wined, dined, and made to feel like a princess. He had taken her to Mauritius for a pre-birthday party only last weekend. But he hadn't said the words. And she wondered why because she had fallen head over heels in love with him.

Now, he had said the words, but there was no marriage proposal. Another thing that had worried her, especially after her uncle mentioned to her a few weeks ago, that he wondered why Usi had not mentioned paying the bride price, especially after he had told her uncle at the onset that he was willing to wait no more than six months before marrying her. Her uncle had asked if there was a chance he may have changed his mind. She had not thought so.

She had fulfilled all expectations and learning from his mother and Mrs Agbi, she had mastered the responsibilities of being the chief priest's wife. The mistake of appearing before Usi during her time did not happen again.

During her time, she stayed away from his quarters and locked the secret door to hers to prevent his entrance. She ate her meals separately from him, and they travelled in separate cars if they had to attend a function. Without being asked, she had removed all black clothing from her wardrobe. It was not such a hard life. She accepted and embraced it because she loved Usi and wanted to be with him; in her estimation, it was a small price to pay. He was worth it.

She shoved the proposal matter to the far reaches of her mind. He had told her he loved her, and if she were patient, a proposal would follow.

The morning was busy. She had a breakfast fit for a queen, served in bed. As she ate, Usi piled up her presents so she could open them when she was done. The man was impossible.

Tiyan rolled her eyes. "Usi, this is too much!"

"Stop complaining," he chided. "It's one birthday present for each year you didn't celebrate your birthday."

If she thought he was done making up for her lost birthday years, she was wrong. When she finally went downstairs to commence greeting her guests, she realised the caterers had arranged eleven cakes.

She turned to Usi in utter amazement, and he shrugged. "There's a cake for each year you didn't celebrate." He kissed her before she could protest.

The party turned out to be amazing. Tiyan was determined

to enjoy herself and put aside thoughts of the absent proposal, even when some guests inquired, "When are you two getting married?"

Then, in the middle of the party, she discovered a gold and diamond solitaire engagement ring while eating her dessert. She knew instinctively that it was hers. Without thinking, she leapt in the air, screaming for joy and waving her hand so everyone could see the ring. Usi stepped forward at that moment and assumed a posture on bended knee.

"You are my world, Tiyan. I love you. Will you marry me?" he asked her in front of the guests, who comprised their family and friends.

Yes! It was a proposal like no other. Better than she had expected.

"Yes!" Tiyan screamed, sensing an overwhelming urge to burst into tears. Her love for this man was boundless; he brought her immense happiness.

Usi rose to his feet, slipped the ring on her finger and kissed her deeply and passionately, not minding the guests who looked on.

Later that night, after the last of the guests had left and the musicians and caterers and interior decorators had cleared up, Usi and Tiyan lay cuddled on the wicker sofa on his bedroom balcony, watching the sleeping city below.

They held each other for a long time, each enjoying the warmth of the other and neither speaking.

"You are aware that I love you, right?" Usi broke the silence after a while.

Tiyan angled her head so she could look into his eyes. "How can I doubt it?" She reached up and touched her lips to his. "You've made me fall in love with you so much it's scary. It's all like a dream. That proposal was out of this world." She raised her left hand and looked at her engagement ring for the nth time that day.

Usi held her hand and kissed it. "I was so scared this would end up in the wrong person's dessert. And even more nervous when Eki said if she found it in hers, she would keep it."

Tiyan chuckled. Yes, that sounded like Eki, all right.

"It's not funny," Usi said. "I was almost having a nervous breakdown thinking about how that would ruin the perfect proposal I had planned. And Osad and Edosa thought it was funny that the chief priest didn't know where the ring was."

Tiyan laughed even more loudly.

"I am glad you have something to laugh about," he grumbled, and unrepentantly, Tiyan shook with laughter.

"Aww. I'm sorry you had such a hard time with the

proposal, my love." Tiyan cradled his face and kissed him.

"You don't sound or look sorry," he said, and she laughed again.

Usi couldn't help but laugh along with her, even though he tried to resist. Their laughter slowly faded, leaving a sense of warmth between them as they began to discuss their plans for their traditional marriage ceremony. They had been living together for more than six months and had no desire to wait any longer before getting married.

The next day, she and Usi visited her uncle to let him know they were ready for the traditional rites that would make them a married couple. Her uncle had witnessed the proposal at her party, and he said he was confident she was ready to take on the role of Usi's wife. They agreed on a date for the wedding: it would be in five weeks.

Just as Usi had pulled out all the stops at her birthday party, he did the same at their wedding. She was marrying a very wealthy man, and he made it clear as he provided the cash for anything and everything required.

Then came the big day, and while Tiyan should have been excited, she woke up that morning with mixed feelings. She was back at home with her uncle and aunt. Except this time, it wasn't the old house where she had grown up with Eki and Amenze, who lived next door. Eki's husband, Oba Osad Ehigie, who was now deeply in love with her, had constructed a large house for her parents in the upscale neighbourhood of Benin.

It was a house befitting their status as the queen's parents. Tiyan had not moved with them to the house, as she had already been living with Usi. It was her first night in the house. She had a room in the house, as did Eki and Eki's older sisters, Eseosa and Aiai.

The room was gorgeous, and she couldn't help but fall in love with it. It was comforting to know that she would always have a place in her uncle's home after she married, but as the hours drew close to her wedding, she was reminded of the family she had lost: her father, mother and brother. She would give anything for them to be there with her to see her marry the man she loved and who loved her back. And though she would go to the ends of the earth to bring them back, she had to confront the harsh truth that they were gone forever and would never return.

On the morning of her wedding, she woke up with a sense of discouragement. Her heart sank as she gazed out her window, observing the bustling activity downstairs. She should not be here but in her father's home. Her father should be giving her to Usi and not her uncle. She remembered the times she had talked with her father about her perfect wedding. Not once had he told her he would not be there to give her away.

He always spoke passionately about the moment when Osamu would sit beside him as they performed the sacred traditional rites for her marriage. But here she was, about to get married in a few hours, and neither her father nor Osamu was here to give her away.

She turned away from the window as she heard a knock on the door.

"Come in," she called.

Almost immediately, the door opened, and Aunt Ayi breezed into the room, looking radiant in an Ankara boubou gown. Clutched in her hands was a mysterious jewellery box. Her hair had already been done in the *okuku* hairstyle, and she was smiling.

"Good morning, Aunt Ayi," Tiyan greeted with a forced smile, attempting to conceal the sorrow in her voice and expression.

"Tiyan! My darling girl. The latest Alile bride. Good morning. I hope you slept well?" She placed the jewellery box on the vanity dressing table, sat on the stool, and beckoned to Tiyan, patting the armchair beside the vanity stool.

"These are your mother's coral beads," she said, opening the jewellery box for Tiyan to examine its contents. "I took them from the house after she died, and I have kept them for you ever since. I could have given them to you before now, but I thought your wedding day would be the best time to present them. Your mother and I discussed our daughters wearing our coral beads during their marriage ceremonies. I know your husband is rich and has bought you your own coral beads. But perhaps you would like to wear some of your mother's, keeping her close to you on your special day."

Overcome with emotion and without words, she gave a nod and softly caressed the coral beads nestled in the jewellery box.

Aunt Ayi placed the box on her lap. "Go through the beads and decide what you want to use. They are yours now. I will send in the women who have arrived to do your *okuku* hairstyle and makeup."

When her aunt left the room, Tiyan locked the door behind her. Still holding her mother's jewellery box, she sank to the floor and began to sob. She had cried in the past, but not like this. She heard knocks on the door and people calling out her name, but she continued to cry and refused to open the door. She lost track of time but could tell from the sound of cars outside that wedding guests had begun to arrive.

Eki and Amenze approached the door and attempted to speak with her. She remained unmoved. Her uncle Zogie arrived at the door and pleaded with her, but she ignored him. She longed for her father, mother, and big brother, Osamu. If she couldn't have them, she preferred to be left alone in her own pity party.

Tiyan was fully aware that she was being unreasonable, but she was consumed by grief and couldn't bring herself to care. She was grieving because on the happiest day of her life, the people she loved the most were absent. Taken from her grasp forever by the icy grip of death.

CHAPTER FOURTEEN

"With all due respect, Chief Isekhure, I don't think you should go into her bedroom."

Usi looked at Chief Alile and restrained his anger. What did the man mean by saying he shouldn't go into Tiyan's bedroom? He arrived about half an hour ago with the king, his mother, brother, elders in his father's house and almost all the chiefs in the kingdom. Upon arrival, he was called away from the marquee tent, where the traditional drummers and dancers entertained the guests as they all waited for the bride's entrance, which would mark the ceremony's commencement.

Chief Alile led him into the main reception of the house and informed him that his bride, who should be ready to be brought out to him by now, was not yet dressed. She had locked herself in her bedroom and was crying, refusing to emerge or let anyone in. Chief Alile had tried everything to get Tiyan to open the door, including threats to break it down, but nothing had worked. Clearly, Chief Alile had lost control of the situation. He wanted to intervene, yet he was being prevented.

"With all due respect, Chief Alile, it doesn't seem like you have the situation in hand. Please lead me to Tiyan's bedroom."

Chief Alile complied, and they walked out of the sitting

room, up the grand stairs, and through a hall filled with elegantly dressed women and bridesmaids waiting to assist Tiyan. Usi greeted them all, including the heavily pregnant queen sitting in a chair just outside the door and looking exasperated. Beside her, Amenze stood looking troubled.

Usi frowned as he seemed to have a déjà vu moment. Only days before, he had received a clear revelation from the gods: a Benin woman, born to be Olori of the Warri Kingdom. He had seen her face but couldn't decipher who it was at the time. Now, as his gaze fell on Amenze, he knew instinctively that she was the one. He was compelled to share the news with her. But now was neither the time nor the place. His house was on fire, and he had to put that fire out first.

He immediately pushed Amenze out of his thoughts and focused entirely on Tiyan and the pressing issue at hand.

"Did anything happen to upset her?" Usi asked Chief Alile just before he knocked on the door.

"No," Chief Alile shook his head. "Nothing happened."

"Well, actually, I think it may be something I did." Mrs Alile looked uncomfortable as she spoke from behind her husband who turned to look at her. "I gave her the coral beads that belonged to her mother. I thought she might want to wear some of them for this happy occasion, but looking back now, I don't think that was a wise thing to do."

"There's nothing wrong in giving her the beads, Mum. The real problem is that all these years, you and Dad never let her grieve properly." Queen Eki sounded annoyed.

"We didn't know any better," Mrs Alile looked from Eki to Usi. "We feared she might be overcome with grief and will herself to die."

"Well, all of this doesn't matter now. I'll go in and talk to her," Usi said.

Chief Alile cleared his throat. "Chief Isekhure, I want you to consider what you are about to do. Traditional dictates–"

"Chief Alile," Usi began in a voice that brooked no arguments. "I am tradition."

Chief Alile bowed slightly and moved away from the door.

"Tiyan!"

Tiyan jumped. The voice from the other side of the door was sharp and sounded angry.

"Usi?" she asked.

Usi was here? Usi had arrived? Had time gone past that quickly?

"T, I am not going to threaten to break down the door as others have," he said, his voice remaining steady as if he was struggling to control his simmering anger. "I will ask you once to open the door, and let's talk like sensible adults. If you don't open it, I am leaving and won't return."

Was Usi threatening her? Usi had never threatened her before. He was always so kind and empathetic, going out of his way to fulfil her every desire.

She walked to the door and opened it. Without a word, Usi stepped in and shut the door behind him, turning the key in the lock.

"You're not dressed," he stated the obvious.

She said nothing but moved to the edge of the bed and sat down.

"I don't know what this drama is about or why you're doing this. But this I know. I am done. I am not going to force you to marry me." He turned and walked towards the door, and Tiyan moved quickly and planted herself between him and the door.

"Don't leave me, please!" The desperation in her voice melted Usi's heart. As she saw his expression soften, her relief was so great that her emotions overflowed, and tears started streaming down her face.

"Oh, you silly, silly, girl!" He picked her up in his arms and walked to the edge of the bed where he sat and cradled her in his arms as she cried.

"I am sorry. I didn't mean to be such a drama queen or embarrass you. I miss my daddy, and my mummy and Osamu. It hurts, Usi. It hurts, here." She took his hand and placed it gently over her heart.

"I know, baby, I know." He crooned as one would to a child.

Her tears began to ebb as he held her in his arms, and she felt calmer.

"Don't leave me," she pleaded.

"Never!" he declared fiercely, holding her tight. "I was only bluffing. I could never leave you. I love you. You know that."

"I know. I love you too."

He cradled her face in his hands, so she looked into his eyes. "So, will you let the women come in and get you dressed?"

"Yes," she whispered.

"Good girl," he said and kissed her lips. It was supposed to be chaste, but as soon as their lips met, it quickly became a hot, hungry kiss. "I want you so much. I can't wait another day."

"I feel the same."

He smiled and dropped a kiss on her forehead. "But you know the rules. You can't have me until you're my wife. And if you delay any longer, we may leave here without becoming man and wife."

Tiyan jumped out of his lap. "I'll hurry," she assured him.

"That's my girl." Usi smiled. "I'll send the women in," he informed her as he stood to his feet and strode towards the door.

An hour later, Tiyan was brought out into the marquee amid singing, dancing, and drumming. It was a beautiful procession of young women and girls in their red long-sleeve mermaid dresses made from luxurious embroidered lace fabric. Their hair was styled in the traditional Benin *okuku* hairstyle, and coral beads covered their hair, neck, and wrists. They all looked resplendent.

Amenze led the procession, and again, Usi had that déjà vu moment. Indeed, it was her. He took his eyes off her and let them rest on Tiyan. The bride, his bride, was, by far, the most beautiful in the procession. She wore a bustier-style red mermaid dress with gold embroidered over one-half of the top of her dress. The bottom of her dress comprised multiple layers of velvet, organza, and ostrich feathers, arranged in a tiered sweetheart pleat ruffles style, and the train appeared to go on forever.

Her *okuku* hairstyle was enriched with red coral beads and gold decorative hair ornaments; her neck and wrists were beautifully adorned with red coral beads. The makeup on her face had been expertly applied, so as Usi rose and took the red organza veil off her face, there was no sign she had been crying. Her beauty was so captivating that it made his heart race.

Tiyan found the ceremony to pass quickly and in a blur. She was in a haze and unaware of the happenings, except when she was placed on Usi's lap and officially declared his wife according to Benin's native law and customs.

"Now, I get to punish you properly for making me suffer earlier today," he whispered in her ear and playfully bit her earlobe.

When it was time for her to leave his lap so the ceremony could continue, Usi refused and held on to her for a few more minutes, causing laughter among the guests.

Once the ceremony concluded, Usi departed for his home, where a second celebration was held. The bride was formally escorted by her friends and family. An hour after he got home, Tiyan and her bridal party arrived, and the celebration continued late into the night.

Amenze led the procession as Tiyan was formally led into her matrimonial home. The longer he gazed upon her, the more certain he was that she was the person he had glimpsed in his dream. She was the one who was crowned Olori of the Warri Kingdom—a Benin woman born for the Warri throne.

Later that night, Usi finally had a chance to speak to Amenze. He pursued her to the car park and shared the revelation with her. She was upset, fearing that she would be forced to marry the elderly king, Olu Ginuwa III, who was in his early seventies. He would have disabused her mind, but that would have led him to share a revelation that was not his place to share.

The revelation of the one who was the rightful heir to the Warri throne and who would be Amenze's husband was not his to share. That duty was for his colleague, the Chief Priest of the Warri Kingdom, Chief Ayo Esigbone. Sharing such a revelation would be crossing a line and have dire consequences.

As he returned to the house, he halted in his tracks and turned to look as the taillights of Amenze's car vanished from sight. He sighed and shook his head. She was angry and driving furiously, and he perceived it would not end well. He looked up at the sky and immediately noticed clouds gathering.

The rain would be welcome to bring some coolness, but this was not a sign that it was about to rain. This was a sign that trouble lay ahead. She was going to mess this up. It was imminent. He made a mental note to offer prayers for her as soon as he returned from his honeymoon.

"Hello, husband," Tiyan called out from the balcony of his bedroom, where she stood watching the guests depart. From there, they could hear laughter, chatting, and music from the grounds.

"Hello, wife." Usi came up behind her, wrapped his arms around her waist and pulled her close, kissing the soft flesh behind her ear and inhaling her sweet fragrance. "You won't believe it if I told you how much I've yearned for this moment."

Tiyan wriggled her backside. "I think I have an idea."

"Witch," Usi groaned, and she giggled. He put her away from him and spun her around to face him.

"Have I told you how beautiful you look today?"

"I think you did when you took off my veil at the start of the ceremony. Still, it never tires me to hear it. Say it again."

"You are the most beautiful woman in this kingdom, Mrs Isekhure."

"If Chief Isekhure says so, then it must be true."

"You know it, babe." He pulled her into his arms and kissed her neck before pulling back. "I have a surprise for you."

"Again?" she asked. "You've given me too many gifts, Usi. You need to stop."

Usi placed a finger over her lips to silence her. "I like spoiling you. And I can afford to. So quit complaining and enjoy receiving my gifts. Your enjoyment makes me happy."

"Okay." Tiyan leaned forward and kissed him. "What is it?"

"You promise you're not going to cry?" Usi asked. "After this morning, I don't know if it's a good time to give you this. It seemed a good idea when I ordered it."

Tiyan frowned. "What is it, Usi?"

"Shut your eyes," Usi ordered. "And no peeking."

Tiyan did as she was told, a smile forming on her lips. Usi moved his wrapper aside to access the cargo shorts he wore beneath. He reached into the side pocket and pulled out a blue velvet jewellery box. He opened the box and turned to Tiyan.

"Okay. Now you can open your eyes."

Tiyan gasped as she saw the gold necklace with the oval locket pendant. As she took it out and looked at it, she realised it was a four-photo locket. Usi's picture was the first, followed by her dad's, mom's, and Osamu's.

"Now you get to carry the ones you love wherever you go."

Tiyan nodded as she struggled with the tears filling her eyes. "Please put it on for me." She turned around so Usi could clasp the necklace around her neck.

"Do you like it?"

"You can't tell?" She raised the locket and kissed it. "Thank you, Usi. I am never taking this off."

"I'm glad you like it. I wasn't sure after this morning."

"No. It's perfect. All my favourite people in one place." She wrapped her arms around him again. "Oh, Usi. You sure know how to make this girl happy."

"Tears were not the reaction I was going for." Usi wrapped his arms around her and held her tight.

"They are happy tears, Usi," Tiyan assured him.

Usi sighed and held her tight. "Sure?"

Tiyan nodded. "I never thought I'd be this happy again."

"I'm glad I make you happy. It's all I want to do. It's all I've wanted to do from the first night we met."

"When you snuck into my room." Tiyan laughed through her tears and pulled back to look at her incredible husband.

"I couldn't resist. Your beauty and charm drew me from the Benin Kingdom to the United Kingdom."

"You should consider being a poet, husband dearest." Tiyan kissed him. "Thank you for the necklace and all my wedding and pre-wedding gifts. And it's enough now; I don't want any more."

"Does that mean you don't want to know what I have

planned for our honeymoon?" he teased.

Tiyan paused for a moment like she was in deep thought. "Curiosity seems to be getting the better part of me. What have you planned? You've been very secretive about it."

Usi shrugged. "Only because I want to surprise you."

"I do not doubt that I will be pleasantly surprised."

And she was. The following day, they took the royal jet to Vegas and went to New York, where they had a small civil ceremony with Ima and his girlfriend as their witnesses. The wedding was the surprise Usi had spoken of on their wedding night. And a pleasant surprise it was.

Usi told Tiyan he never wanted her to think he would take another wife. She was all the woman he wanted and needed. Not that she doubted that. Perhaps at the beginning after Esele's lie, but never again. Usi had done everything to ensure that.

With their civil wedding in the bag, they continued their honeymoon by visiting the Maldives again and ended by visiting Monaco and the South of France. It was a delightful experience, and when they returned to Benin, Tiyan was expecting a baby and deeply in love with her husband.

CHAPTER FIFTEEN

Tiyan's mind was in turmoil as she made her way home from the palace following a meeting with Eki, Amenze, and Ede, who was now their new best friend. Something was very wrong with Amenze, and she couldn't quite put her finger on it. Eki and Ede had not noticed, being too wrapped up in trying to connect Amenze with Prince Jimi, the Crown Prince of the Warri Kingdom, who would soon be crowned Olu of Warri following his father's death.

She also did not perceive a problem during the meeting, being too worried about Eki and Ede flouting Usi's explicit instructions to Amenze. Apparently, on their wedding day, Usi had told Amenze that she would be Olori of the Warri Kingdom. He had also asked her not to do anything to mess it up and not to try to make it happen.

Ede and Eki were bent on introducing Amenze to Prince Jimi. An appointment had been made for Amenze to have dinner with the prince in his home in Warri in a few days. Ede and Eki thought their actions could not be classified as trying to make it happen. Tiyan tried to talk them out of it, but no one listened to her. She sat in that meeting worried about what she viewed as the total disregard for her husband's office as the Chief Priest of the Benin Kingdom.

She knew their actions would have consequences and was terrified about how it would end. But what bothered her even more now was that Amenze did not look happy. She was getting the support of her friends to get the man Usi prophesied she would marry, so it begged the question, why wouldn't she be thrilled?

Something was going on with Amenze that she wasn't saying. And possibly because she thought her friends were now married and too wrapped up in their spouses and marriages to be concerned with her deepest worries.

Tiyan sighed as she indicated left and turned the steering of her white Range Rover Evoque vehicle toward the private road leading up to Usi's home—her new home as Mrs Usi Isekhure. Her new life was still a dream. Usi spoilt her. Nothing was too much for him to do for her.

The man was good to her and good for her. There was no doubt in her heart that she had married the best man in the world. She adored him, and she loved her new life with him. He was her compensation for losing her family—and what a compensation he was.

As she brought the vehicle to a halt in front of the house and handed the key to a driver who would park it in the car park, she took her mind off Amenze and her other friends and prepared to spend a blissful evening with her husband. He would be home by now, as dinner would soon be served.

"Where are you coming from?"

The coldness in Usi's voice caused Tiyan to pause midway through putting down her handbag. She turned slowly in the middle of her dressing room and came face-to-face with Usi, as she had never seen him before. The secret door connecting her dressing room with his suite of rooms was ajar, and he stood in the doorway, hands on hip, wearing a red wrapper, red traditional short-sleeve shirt, red shoes, and red coral beads. He looked stern and reminded her of the day she'd rushed out to greet him while it was her time. Well, it wasn't her time, and wouldn't be for many months as she was pregnant, so why did he look so stern?

What was this about? She wondered. *What was going on?*

She licked her lips as they suddenly felt dry. "Usi, what-?"

"Answer the question, T. Where are you coming from?"

"I went to the palace to see Eki."

"And?" He was waiting for more.

Tiyan placed her large bucket bag on the chest of drawers and turned to face him once more. "What is this, Usi?" she asked. "Am I not allowed to visit Eki?"

She visited the palace nearly every day after their honeymoon, especially since Eki had given birth to a son, Prince Aimua, during her and Usi's absence. It had never been a problem.

"Answer my question." His tone was quiet but authoritative.

Tiyan sighed. She knew where this was going. Eki had told her, "Don't disclose anything to your husband, the chief priest."

Usi knew her actions even before she had the chance to tell him. He didn't consistently fuss over them. Occasionally, he would playfully tease her for attempting to conceal things he already knew from him, and together, they would laugh about it. But this was different. He wasn't laughing, and she knew why. She took another deep breath.

"Amenze was there. And Ede was there. And as you already know, there is an arrangement for Amenze to meet with Prince Jimi, whom she's prophesied to marry."

"She's prophesied to marry Prince Jimi?" Usi asked like it was news to him.

"Usi, don't play dumb right now. You know she's prophesied to marry Prince Jimi!"

"Yeah?" Usi asked, folding his arms across his chest. "And who gave her that prophecy?"

Tiyan stomped her foot angrily. Oh, enough of this nonsense! "You did!"

Usi wagged a finger at her. "Do not tell lies against me!"

he snapped. "You'd be in much trouble now if you weren't my wife! I did not tell Amenze she would marry Prince Jimi. I told her she was Olori, and the Olu of Warri crowned her so."

Tiyan threw her arms up in the air. "Well, it's the same thing, isn't it?" She asked, feeling a little frustrated. "Prince Jimi is the next Olu of Warri!"

"And who told you that? Because I certainly didn't!"

Tiyan froze. Now, her husband had her full undivided attention. Her heart raced in her chest, quickening with every passing moment. "What do you mean? Is Prince Jimi not the next Olu of Warri?"

"I cannot answer that question," Usi said quietly. "Who will ascend the throne of the Warri Kingdom as king is not for the Chief Priest of the Benin Kingdom to reveal even if he knows it. So, no. I cannot tell you who the next Olu of Warri Kingdom is. But I can tell you how Amenze's meeting Prince Jimi will play out."

Tiyan watched silently as Usi walked out of her dressing room and into his quarters. She followed him like one in a dream until they reached his private sitting room, where he gestured for her to sit.

"Your friend Amenze reminds me of Shakespeare's Macbeth," Usi said as he sat in an armchair across the room from

Tiyan.

"What does that mean?" Tiyan asked wearily.

Usi observed his wife intently. "Dear wife, a prophecy revealed is like a two-edged sword. It can be a blessing, or it can be a curse. When I read Macbeth for the first time as a young teenager, I couldn't help but think he would have been better off not knowing he would be king. I believe the same is true in Amenze's case. In telling her she would be queen, it appears I have set her on a path to self-destruction."

Tiyan's chest felt as though it was being squeezed tightly. "What do you mean?"

Usi propped his feet up on the footstool and reclined in his chair. "I have another prophecy. She is going to visit Prince Jimi and will be wined and dined and drugged and raped. That singular act will cause her to be rejected by the gods of the land. The gods of this land and the gods of the land of Warri. She will not be queen. Although the Olu of Warri loves her, the powers behind the throne will not allow him to marry her and remain the Olu. At best, she will go down in history as a victim, one of the women raped by Prince Jimi Tunoka."

Tiyan sprang up and placed both hands on her head. She was greatly distressed. "Usi, please do–"

"Please sit down, T. I am not done. The prophecy would

have been a blessing if she had left it alone and lived her life, allowing it to come to fruition in its own time and in its own way. I warned her not to mess it up. I told her not to try to make it happen. But she didn't listen. And when people don't heed instructions, there are consequences. She didn't tell you, possibly because she isn't entirely sure. But she is pregnant."

Tiyan's hands instinctively flew to cover her mouth as she collapsed back onto the sofa. Could this be the reason Amenze had not looked completely happy? Was she pregnant? Was she pregnant by the smooth-talking Bawo? How would she ever fulfil the prophecy while carrying another man's child? Oh, it was a mess. Also, what prophecy was there to fulfil? Usi already countered it. He said–

Tiyan couldn't bring herself to recollect what Usi said. Oh no! Amenze!

"The pregnancy is not an issue," Usi carried on, oblivious to her distress. As he talked, his gaze was fixed on the wall behind her as if it held the key to his next words. "The pregnancy is not what stops her from becoming Olori. Let's be clear. What stops her from becoming Olori is that Prince Jimi sleeps with her. Whether forcefully or consensually is irrelevant. Once that happens, she can no longer be queen. She will no longer be able to marry the man responsible for her pregnancy. He will believe it is Jimi's. She will live out her days as a single, unwed mother.

She should have listened to me and left the prophecy alone."

Tiyan felt ill. "Usi, is there something you can do?"

"Ah!" Usi leaned in, resting his chin on his hand as he closely scrutinised Tiyan. "Now, you want Chief Isekhure to fix it, yes?"

Tiyan nodded, her eyes imploring him.

"You want Chief Isekhure to fix it as he fixed the little problem with Eki the last time, right?"

Tiyan nodded again.

"No, T, I won't do it." He sat back in his chair. "You sat in that meeting and allowed your friends to flaunt my orders as if they didn't matter. Now, they will learn the hard way that my instructions are the exact words of the gods and must not be disobeyed."

Tiyan massaged her temple, trying to soothe the throbbing pain. This turned out to be much more severe than she had first anticipated. Usi's refusal to help her was unprecedented.

"Usi, I am sorry. I did try to tell them not to proceed with the plan, but they said it was just a small meeting."

Usi shook his head. "A meeting that will lead to Amenze being drugged and raped and change the course of her life can't be a small meeting."

"But Usi. We didn't know any of this."

"You organised a meeting for your friend with a man none of you know anything about? Prince Jimi is notorious for spiking his friends' drinks with drugs. He has been accused of drugging women and then sleeping with them. Thanks to his father's abundant wealth from oil-rich Warri, he has yet to pay for his crimes. The women are paid to be quiet."

Tiyan groaned. "I didn't like this from the get-go."

Usi shrugged, unperturbed. "Then you should have insisted that they don't do it. I don't understand the deal with Amenze. When I gave her the prophecy, she looked furious, like she would beat me on the head with a stick if I weren't Chief Priest Isekhure. Next, she's planning a trip to Warri to beg Prince Jimi to marry her. Is she so desperate for marriage?"

Tiyan sighed, knowing that Usi couldn't grasp what was happening with Amenze when she didn't fully comprehend it herself. "She's not desperate for marriage. She recently experienced a broken heart. and I don't think she's thinking properly about her actions."

"When she's a single, unwed mother, she will have plenty of time to consider her actions. Hindsight, they say, is always twenty-twenty vision."

Tiyan rose from the sofa, approached Usi, and settled

onto his lap, gently holding his face in her hands. "My husband, the one who holds my heart. I know you're upset, and rightly so. You gave instructions, but Amenze didn't follow them. Instead of listening to you, she chose to listen to Eki, Ede, and me. I didn't protest enough, so I am as much to blame. But please forgive her. Forgive me. Forgive us all, and please fix this. I asked before, and you fixed it, and I am asking again. Please."

Usi gazed at his wife for a long moment, and although it pained him, he shook his head. "No. I will not fix it." He averted his gaze, unable to bear the sight of her devastated expression. "It will happen, as I have said. Not that I need to prophesy where Prince Jimi is concerned. Put Jimi and a beautiful woman together, and there will be sex, consensual or not. I don't need to be the mouthpiece of the gods to declare that."

"Usi, darling –"

"T, drop it. I've had a long day in the main shrine and I'm exhausted and hungry. Let's go downstairs. Mrs Agbi should have dinner ready by now."

Tiyan rose to her feet with a quiet resignation. "I'll freshen up and meet you downstairs in a bit."

As Tiyan stood in front of the mirror in her dressing room, retouching her makeup, she considered what Usi had said. How could she have let Eki and Ede take matters into their own hands like that? Why didn't she insist they let the prophecy be and watch it unfold without doing anything about it? Why was it necessary for Amenze to meet Prince Jimi? Prince Jimi wasn't likely to be king as Usi had suggested, and even if he was, did Amenze want to marry a man notorious for using drugs and raping women?

If Prince Jimi was known for such evil, how had it missed their attention? Ede was acquainted with him. Did she know about his reputation? Did Amenze know? Tiyan had never been interested in learning about the Warri Kingdom and the Tunoka royal family. But if Amenze were interested in marrying the man, she ought to have discovered something about him. And was she willing to go forward because she thought Prince Jimi was her husband as he would be the next Olu of Warri?

Suppose she discovered that Prince Jimi very likely would not be king. Would she reconsider and abort this accursed mission? Tiyan looked at the top of the vanity dressing table where her phone lay. Aborting this cursed mission was only a phone call away.

All she had to do was call Amenze and tell her about Prince Jimi, adding that Jimi would not be king. Indeed, that was enough. But would that be wise? Usi had not asked her to divulge any of the information he had shared with her. But, then again, Usi had not asked her not to divulge any of the information he'd shared with her.

Tiyan took a deep breath and reached for her phone with

a shaky hand. She dialled Amenze's number. As the phone rang, she glanced up and caught sight of Usi in the mirror, still clad in that dreadful red outfit.

"Amenze, let me call you back much later." She cut the call as Amenze answered and put down her phone. Ignoring Usi, she picked up her lipstick and raised it to her lips.

"You gain nothing by trying to warn her. She will go for that appointment. Right now, she is on the path to destruction and is like a dog set to be lost that will no longer heed the voice of its owner."

He turned to walk away, but Tiyan cleared her throat, causing him to pause and turn to look at her.

"Please don't wear that dreadful attire to dinner."

He grinned. "Of course," he said and walked away.

Usi kissed Tiyan's head and smiled as she mumbled unintelligibly in her sleep. She was his world. He would do anything for her and for the babies they were expecting. Twins. A boy and a girl that would complete their family. He'd seen it but not told her yet, wanting her to find out from the doctors and the scan at the appropriate time. He knew the issue with Amenze troubled her. But he couldn't jump in and save the day as he had done last time. It was time her friends learnt that there were consequences for their actions.

Eki was queen and possibly didn't appreciate the sacrifice it took to get her married to Osad. He had taken a considerable risk in discharging her from the hospital without her taking the virginity test. If it had backfired, he would have been in much trouble. Thankfully, when Osad found out, it didn't matter much, as he was already in love with Eki. Otherwise, there would have been hell to pay.

At the time, Tiyan worried about Eki and herself and the problem that would come to her door if anything went wrong. No one considered what would happen to him. For years, his ancestors had held the position of chief priest in this land. It was a sensitive role, and one's loyalty was always with the king and no one else. In intervening as he had, he shifted loyalty from the king to Eki, all because of Tiyan.

Anyone would have thought a lesson would be learnt. But no. Eki quickly forgot how she almost, with her own hands, ruined the prophecy he and his father had given her. Now, she was set to mislead Amenze and send her down a path of no return. And to get involved in this issue would mean going outside his jurisdiction.

He would be entering the Warri kingdom. It was a dangerous move. If he appeased the gods of Benin, how did he appease the gods of Warri? It would be hazardous. It could lead to trouble between the two kingdoms and his removal from the chief priest's office. In attempting to help Amenze, he could throw away something his family had held for hundreds of years. He could be banished from Benin forever, along with his descendants. More importantly, he could be struck dead.

Tiyan didn't understand these risks. When he began dating her, he tried to shield her from much truth about the office he held and what was expected of him. He had done so because he feared she would be overwhelmed and flee. Yes. The gods had approved her to be his wife, but she could reject him and leave the marriage if she thought she couldn't cope with the reality of being the wife of a chief priest.

For this reason, he tried not to share much about his work with her and refused her initiation into being a priestess. She was called priestess, but it was more honorary for being his wife. In the real sense of the word, she was no priestess. She couldn't cope with that world, and he wouldn't scare her away by showing it to her.

He reviewed with his mother and Mrs Agbi even the things she should have learnt as the chief priest's wife. She would learn them in small bits, in phases, as they journeyed together in their marriage. He wrapped his arm tightly about her as he shut his eyes and drifted off to sleep.

CHAPTER SIXTEEN

Even before Tiyan rolled across the large bed to Usi's side, she knew she would find it empty and cold, an indication that he had long woken up and left home. The last few days, he'd been leaving home early and coming home late. She knew he was busy with a community dispute, which had led to the loss of lives, but she also wondered if he was taking advantage of it to avoid her, leaving before she rose and not returning until she was fast asleep.

She hadn't had the chance to talk to him again about the issue with Amenze, which bothered her as the days passed. Tomorrow, Amenze would travel to Warri for her doomed meeting with Prince Jimi. As Tiyan dragged herself out of bed, she couldn't shake off the feeling of misery that engulfed her.

Nonetheless, she braced herself for the day ahead. She had quite a bit on her itinerary for the day. She wanted to call in at the bakery and chat with the manager and staff as was her daily practice. She would probably also spend some time with the manager going through last month's record of financial transactions. After that, she planned to go to the palace.

Yesterday, while on a conference call with Eki and Amenze, she briefly mentioned the possibility of a pitch event and trade fair for Elevate in Benin. Elevate was a concept originally created by Eki to bring Benin entrepreneurs and investors together.

The pitch event and trade fair she proposed would be quite unlike the two pitch events held thus far. It would be a three-day event that would attract Benin entrepreneurs and investors from major cities in West Africa. It was her brainchild, which she conceived while on her honeymoon. Eki and Amenze agreed it was a brilliant idea and were on board. They arranged to meet today at the queen's residence in the palace to discuss the plan in detail.

Tiyan looked forward to the meeting and to seeing Amenze again, especially after her discussion with Usi the other night. As she recollected the conversation, she was again deeply troubled. She couldn't get over Usi's new prophecy of what would befall Amenze in Prince Jimi's home. She also couldn't get over the fact that Amenze was pregnant.

As they discussed Elevate later that morning, Tiyan watched Amenze closely, and she could tell that while pretending to be happy, Amenze was anything but happy. The realisation broke Tiyan's heart. Several times, she wanted to ask Amenze if anything was bothering her, but she didn't know if that would help or hurt her. Also, she feared that if she opened her mouth, she would be unable to stop herself from blurting out the whole truth and begging her dear friend not to make the trip to Warri to see Prince Jimi.

Ede arrived a couple of hours later to spend her lunch break with them, wearing a huge smile.

"Hey, baby girl, ready for your big date tomorrow?" She sat on the sofa beside Amenze and dropped a little gift bag on her lap. "A little something from Dizola for you to wear tomorrow. Nothing like sexy underwear to help boost a woman's confidence."

Ede was a businesswoman who designed and manufactured her own women's lingerie line. She was successful, and her designs were in shops selling luxury goods for women across Africa, Europe, and America.

Amenze looked shocked as she pulled out a sheer one-piece of silk and lace underwear in a nude colour from the bag.

"Oh, my, Ede. That is one sexy underwear," Eki said, leaning over and taking the underwear from Amenze's hands.

Amenze smiled at Ede. "Yes, it's beautiful. Thank you."

"Anything for you, baby girl," Ede responded and hugged Amenze.

"I think this is the courage boost you need, Amenze," Eki said and turned to look at Tiyan. "What do you think, Cousin T?"

"It's beautiful," Tiyan mumbled.

"What's your deal?" Eki sounded annoyed. "You've been wearing a long face all morning like you're at a funeral. Problems with the husband?"

Tiyan feigned a smile. "None that I know of. It's probably just my pregnancy affecting my mood. But pay no attention to me." She looked at Amenze. "It's a beautiful underwear. Dizola makes beautiful lingerie, and I should know, as Ede gifted me a few before my honeymoon. Usi swoons over them."

Eki rolled her eyes, and Ede and Amenze giggled.

"Are you still nervous?" Ede asked Amenze.

Amenze smiled faintly. "A little."

Tiyan bit back a groan. She wanted to grab Amenze and shake some sense into her. If she was feeling nervous, wasn't that a sign she shouldn't go on the date?

"You will be fine," Eki assured her, leaning over and dropping the lingerie back into the gift bag on Amenze's lap. "Now, you have this sexy lingerie, and you also have my earlier advice of getting some Dutch courage."

Once again, Tiyan bit back a groan. She could see Prince Jimi lacing Amenze's alcohol with drugs. Amenze would be unable to get behind the wheel to drive home, and she would sleep over, and Prince Jimi would –

Without thinking, her hand flew over her mouth to stifle

an involuntary sob.

Eki instantly turned to her. "What is wrong with you today?"

"One moment, I need to use the bathroom." Tiyan rose and fled in the direction of the guest bathroom.

In the quiet of the bathroom, Tiyan took a deep breath. It was time she raised the issue of Prince Jimi's questionable character. She had spent some time researching Prince Jimi following her chat with Usi the other day, and she had been shocked at the things she had discovered, surprised that she had not known any of those things before.

Usi said talking to Amenze was a lost cause, but she owed it to her friend to tell her what she knew about Prince Jimi. So, just as Ede was preparing to leave after lunch, Tiyan brought up the subject.

"Ede, how well do you know Prince Jimi?" she asked, ignoring Eki, who looked at her like she'd grown two heads. "I ask because I have read some unsavoury things about him."

Ede laughed. "Yes. Jimi's story is all over the internet. He's notorious for having parties that flow with drinks and drugs and for spiking his friends' drinks. And that's not a made-up story. He spiked my drink with an aphrodisiac the only time I attended his party, and if Sato hadn't whisked me away, I have no idea what would have happened."

Tiyan stared at her in utter disbelief. "You know this from personal experience and think it's okay for Amenze to have dinner with him in his home?"

"Ede already told me about Prince Jimi spiking her drink," Amenze said.

Tiyan turned to look at Amenze. "You know that Prince Jimi spiked Ede's drink with an aphrodisiac, and you're still willing to meet him for dinner?"

Amenze shrugged. "People change."

"Yes. That's what I told her. People change," Ede said.

"Is this the reason you've been acting so weird?" Eki asked. "What do you imagine that a man mourning his father is going to do to Amenze? Drug her and rape her? This is not a party. This is a dinner date in his home, with servants and guards. Every one of them is mourning Olu Ginuwa III. Why would Prince Jimi display party-boy behaviour? Besides, she is his wife. Why would he want to drug her to sleep with her?"

Tiyan turned around to look at Amenze. "Are you comfortable with this?"

Before Amenze could respond, Eki said, "Cousin T, the man is her husband. Your husband prophesied it. For that reason alone, I believe she will be fine."

Tiyan opened her mouth to speak but remembered Usi's words and closed them again. It seemed Amenze, like the dog destined for doom, would not heed its owner's voice.

It was almost midnight when Usi entered his home, dragging his tired body up the stairs to his bedroom suite. He had left home early that morning and spent the day in Okada, settling a dispute between two communities at war. He had been doing that for a few days and hoped to reach a decision today, but that was impossible as he had to leave for the main shrine to make some pending sacrifices. He was drained and looked forward to crawling into bed.

When he entered his bedroom, Tiyan was not asleep but sitting on her side of his bed and sobbing. Usi sighed. Not tonight. Especially not tonight. Tonight, he would have given anything to come home and find her fast asleep as it had been the last few days. He instinctively understood the issue without needing to ask, and it pained him deeply to witness her suffering.

"Usi, please, you need to do something. She's going to see Prince Jimi tomorrow. I can't bear for something awful to happen to her. I have read a little about Prince Jimi and asked Ede about it today. It turns out that Ede had a bad experience. Amenze also knows about Ede's experience, which Ede shared with her in London. Eki was there while we talked, and like

Amenze and Ede, she didn't think the revelation about Prince Jimi was sufficient reason to cancel the dinner date."

Usi let out a sigh and scratched his head. "T, drop this issue. Don't cry more than the bereaved. I told you the other day when you attempted to call her that even if you told her the truth, she would not listen. She is on the path to self-destruction, and she won't stop until she's utterly destroyed herself."

"How can I drop this issue, Usi?" Tiyan sobbed. "She is my friend. My best friend from childhood. She is closer than a friend. She is my sister. I can't watch her destroy herself, Usi. I can't sit back and watch her destroy herself. If you won't help her, I will."

Usi laughed. "And how do you plan to do that?"

"I will drive with her to Warri if I have to, and I won't let her out of my sight."

Usi shook his head. "You're talking nonsense, T. And you're not thinking straight. You're upset. Lie down and get some rest. You'll feel better in the morning."

"No! I won't feel better in the morning!" Tiyan cried. "I'll feel worse knowing my friend is closer to her doom."

"T, please drop this issue. I have had a long day and want to shower and go to bed."

"Oh, don't you even want something light to eat? I know

it's late, but you must be hungry. I can go downstairs and fix something or ask one of the maids to get it while I keep you company in the shower." Tiyan dabbed her tears with her fingers.

Usi shook with laughter. "Are you making this offer to get me to fix Amenze's problem?"

"Yes." Tiyan threw her hands up in frustration. "Usi, please!"

Usi shook his head. "I need to shower, T."

He was gone, and Tiyan lay on the large bed crying. When Usi returned to bed, he ignored her, got into his side of the bed, and was out as soon as his head touched the pillow. Tiyan watched him, hardly able to believe he had not even said good night to her, kissed her, or held her as he slept. Was he really sleeping? His steady, rhythmic breathing indicated that he was out for the count.

Usi had a rough night. When he opened his eyes, he instantly knew why. Tiyan was sitting up in bed, silently sobbing. He looked at the digital alarm clock on his bedside table; it was 4:30 am.

"Did you get any sleep, T?" He rubbed his eyes and pushed himself into a sitting position.

Tiyan shook her head, picked up a tissue, and blew loudly

into it before putting the tissue in a heap of tissues on her bedside table. Usi raised a brow.

"Have you been crying all this time?"

It had been four long hours since he finally lay down to rest. Surely, she couldn't have been crying the entire time.

Tiyan nodded and began to sob again. Usi groaned loudly as he reached for her and gathered her up into his arms. Her temperature was up.

"T. Baby, you're making yourself ill. This isn't good for you. And it's not good for the baby."

"I can't help it." Her voice was hoarse and no more than a whisper. "She's my friend. When I went to live with my uncle and aunt after my family died, I was traumatised. I would go to bed and have nightmares. Amenze started coming over to sleep with me. She and Eki would hold me tight when my nightmares would start. And when I would cry, they would cry with me."

She pulled away from him, got out of bed, and left the bedroom. Usi stayed in bed for a few minutes before heading downstairs to the gym. When he was done, he showered, changed into jogger bottoms and a T-shirt, and went looking for her. He still had to go to Okada to finalise the issues with the communities and pass his judgment, but that could wait until later in the day. Right now, he had to attend to his wife.

She lay in her bed, and the bedroom was cloaked in silence. The sobbing had ceased, but she looked unwell. Usi sat on the bed and touched her forehead, frowning as he realised her temperature had risen some more. She did not acknowledge him; she just lay there, gazing into space, and he could tell she was mentally far away. He took her hand in his and kissed it.

"Okay. I'll do it. I'll fix it. But I need you to stop making yourself ill. Please."

She turned her head and locked eyes with him for the first time since he entered the room.

"You'll do it?"

Usi nodded. "I'll do it for you."

Tiyan sat up and threw herself into his arms. "Thank you, Usi." She broke down and began to cry again. "Thank you so much. I'll never ask this of you again, I promise."

Usi held her close, stroking her back as he did. "I did say you have to stop making yourself ill. That's the deal. So far, you're not holding up to your end of the bargain."

Tiyan pulled back to study his face. "These are happy tears," she assured him, wiping the tears with the back of her hand.

"Well, you've shed enough tears for one lifetime in the space of a few hours. No more tears, happy or otherwise."

Tiyan smiled through her tears. "Okay, Usi. No more tears."

He pulled her into his arms and kissed the top of her head. "What am I going to do with you, T?" he muttered. "I need you to lie in today. I will ask Mrs Agbi to serve you breakfast in bed and get a doctor from the palace hospital to come in and see you. Okay?"

Tiyan nodded. She was too tired and too sleepy to argue. She let Usi tuck her in and drifted off to sleep, knowing that he would take care of things like last time and Amenze would be okay.

Moments later, Usi stepped into the shrine wearing his chief priest attire. He picked up a bottle of gin, poured out a libation to the gods and his ancestors, and sat cross-legged on the floor. He could not do this alone and would need his counterpart in the Warri Kingdom. He picked up his phone, lying on the marble floor next to him, and called Chief Ayo Esigbone.

"Usi Isekhure, I greet you," Ayo Esigbone's voice drifted from the other end of the line.

"Good morning, Ayo. How are things in Warri?"

"So-so." Ayo Esigbone responded. "I have been quite busy, with the king joining his ancestors, the *Egbejugbele* priest controversy and the Okere juju festival preparations. It has been a busy time. But I am sure you have not called me at 7 am to discuss my itinerary. What can I do for you, my brother?"

"I have a request to make," Usi said. "It's a small favour, and I will be in your debt if you can assist me."

One hour later, with Usi Isekhure working in tandem with Ayo Esigbone, the appeasement sacrifice was made, the gods of Benin and Warri were appeased, and the prophecy of doom over Amenze was reversed.

EPILOGUE

"Didn't Amenze look extremely happy, my dear?" Tiyan inquired as she settled into bed beside Usi.

The coronation of Ogiame Erejuwa II as the Olu of Warri was a resounding success, marked by an opulent ceremony attended by many. Guests travelled from different countries to be there. The first day's activities ended past midnight, and guests went to bed to rest and prepare for the next day.

Usi and Tiyan had recently entered their bedroom, with only a few hours left to sleep before breakfast and the start of the day's events. At the palace in Ode Itsekiri, the Olu of Warri accommodated a number of kings and their entourages. Accommodations were provided for others in hotels situated in Warri and Ode Itsekiri.

Tiyan and Usi received dual invitations to the coronation as both Amenze's friends and members of the Oba of Benin's entourage. Just like Ede and her husband Sato, who served as Oba Osad's bodyguard. Sato's company, Bulwark, was responsible for providing security for the event. They were all spending the night at the Ode Itsekiri palace, which made it more convenient to attend the next day's activities.

Tiyan found the entire ceremony to be a captivating

showcase of Itsekiri culture. In the morning, a boat regatta and cultural displays were scheduled. She eagerly looked forward to it, thrilled by every aspect of the coronation ceremony.

Seeing her friend Amenze happy brought her the greatest joy. Every time Olu Erejuwa II caught a glimpse of Amenze, Tiyan couldn't help but notice the unmistakable spark of love dancing in his eyes. It was a delight to witness. At last, Eki, Ede, Amenze, and she were all married and not just married, but happily married. Throughout the ceremony, Amenze had a radiant glow.

"Yes. She looked happy," Usi agreed, pulling her close and planting a kiss on her lips.

Tiyan gazed at her husband, contemplating, as she often did, how differently her life might have played out if he hadn't been a part of it. He saved Eki, and by saving her, he had, in effect, saved the entire Alile family. He also saved Amenze.

"Thank you, Usi." Tiyan held his face gently and pressed a kiss to his forehead. "I'm grateful for all that you do for me. There's no one else I would rather have as my husband than you. I couldn't have wished for a more perfect husband. If I had to pick for myself, I couldn't have chosen a better man. You tick all my boxes and then some. I look at what my life has become; I look at Eki and Amenze, who are so happy, and I am grateful to you and grateful for you. You are the consolation for the loss of both my parents and my brother. You truly are a remarkable compensation.

My love for you is immeasurable, surpassing life itself. If I were given another opportunity, I'd choose you all over again. If I come back to this world, I will search tirelessly for you, my husband, lover, friend, soulmate."

Smiling, Usi raised her hand to his lips. "I love you too. You know this. I promise that nothing will ever come between us, not even death. I am dedicated to you for eternity, and I will never leave your side. In my next life, I will search the entire world until I find you, the one who holds my heart, the one my soul longs for, the one who completes me entirely."

As his lips sought and found hers, Tiyan enveloped him in a warm embrace, pulling him tightly against her as if wanting to share every heartbeat. She parted her lips, inviting him in with a subtle tantalising promise. Usi's kiss quickly became more demanding and Tiyan met it with an urgency of her own. Just beyond the threshold of their room, a commotion stirred, breaking the stillness of the moment. Usi broke the kiss and pulled away with a frown.

"Did you hear that noise?" Tiyan asked wondering what could be going on outside their bedroom door. "It sounded like someone screaming."

"There's only one way to find out." Usi got up to investigate, and Tiyan followed him closely behind.

Opening the bedroom door revealed a breathtaking

courtyard with an expansive swimming pool. Standing near the pool, a couple displayed signs of tension through their body language. Tiyan struggled to comprehend the woman's speech, as she spoke in both high tones and the Agbor language. However, she was obviously intoxicated and the man she was with seemed clearly annoyed.

Usi and Tiyan recognised the man as Obi Chez Aboh, King of Agbor. Like them, he was a distinguished guest at the coronation ceremony and was also accommodated overnight at the palace. His posture suggested that he was making an effort to manage his anger. He stood much taller, towering over the angry, drunken woman who seemed to be swearing.

"If you want to make a scene, I am happy to accommodate you," he told his companion.

Usi and Tiyan exchanged glances and quickly retreated into their bedroom, closing the door to avoid being seen by the other couple.

-THE END-

ABOUT ETURUVIE EREBOR

British by birth and Nigerian by descent, Eturuvie 'Evie' Erebor is an inspirational and self-growth speaker, writer, publisher, talk show host, and lawyer. She has written twenty-two books and published her article series, 'Preparing to Cleave', on the Vanguard Newspaper's Christian page in Nigeria between 2004 and 2007. Her articles have also been published in various newsletters and magazines, as well as on FaithWriters.Com.

Since 2004, she's spoken in churches and schools, transforming the lives of women and youth. Due to personal experience, she's determined to add more value to the lives of her fellow women. Hence, she began her initiative, 'DOZ Network'—writing and publishing DOZ Magazine, DOZ Devotional, and DOZ Chronicles, as well as hosting DOZ Show and DOZ Live Inspirational Conference.

A passionate storyteller, she's currently working on stories that appeal to women who are romantics at heart, and aid in her lifelong mission to educate, inspire, and empower with everything she does.

ABOUT DOZ CHRONICLES

DOZ Magazine was created to publish the stories of women, some painful, some joyful but all inspirational. When DOZ Magazine began operations in 2009, our true stories comprised a section within the magazine. However, readers quickly grew tired of reading the stories piece by piece. They came to loathe the phrase "to be continued", so we created an independent magazine dedicated to telling our inspirational stories in their entirety in a series. This magazine was known as the DOZ (True Story) Magazine, which significantly affected readers. It went out of circulation for a few years, but due to popular demand, it returned in 2015 as DOZ Chronicles. Under this title, four novellas were published, namely, DOZ Chronicles: Kemi, DOZ Chronicles: Lara, DOZ Chronicles: Ruki, and DOZ Chronicles: Nneka. They were published under the African Women Narratives series, and each is based on actual events.

The vision of DOZ Chronicles is expanding with its first fiction novel, DOZ Chronicles: Oloi.

www.ingramcontent.com/pod-product-compliance
Lightning Source LLC
La Vergne TN
LVHW041207150826
845673LV00001B/310

* 9 7 8 1 8 3 8 3 8 4 4 6 3 *